"Shut up," Gaia whispered, wrestling Tatiana into submission even as she dangled in the air. "I know you're scared, but you're okay, so lose the skirt."

She waited for Tatiana's body to go limp in agreement and then yanked her through the window. They lay on the floor, Tatiana's breath coming in ragged, panicked gasps, Gaia's as normal as ever. When Tatiana had composed herself, Gaia sat up.

"Can I trust you not to freak out?" she whispered. Tatiana nodded. Gaia stood, silently, and slipped the window shut; then she paused and listened intently to the sounds inside the house. Not even a creak of the building settling. Apparently their little adventure on the fire escape hadn't alerted George to their presence.

Don't miss any books in this thrilling series:

FEARLESS™

#1 *Fearless*
#2 *Sam*
#3 *Run*
#4 *Twisted*
#5 *Kiss*
#6 *Payback*
#7 *Rebel*
#8 *Heat*
#9 *Blood*
#10 *Liar*
#11 *Trust*
#12 *Killer*
#13 *Bad*
#14 *Missing*
#15 *Tears*
#16 *Naked*
#17 *Flee*
#18 *Love*
#19 *Twins*
#20 *Sex*
#21 *Blind*
#22 *Alone*

Available from SIMON PULSE

FEARLESS™

ALONE

FRANCINE PASCAL

SIMON PULSE
New York London Toronto Sydney Singapore

First Simon Pulse edition July 2002

Text copyright © 2002 by Francine Pascal

Cover copyright © 2002 by 17th Street Productions, an Alloy, Inc. company.

SIMON PULSE
An imprint of Simon & Schuster Children's Publishing Division
1230 Avenue of the Americas, New York, NY 10020

 Produced by 17th Street Productions,
an Alloy, Inc. company
151 West 26th Street
New York, NY 10001

Printed in the United States of America
10 9 8 7 6 5 4 3 2 1

Library of Congress Control Number: 2002101034
ISBN: 0-7434-4400-0

To Emily Groopman

Here are some facts I learned from my dad, back when I still had a dad.

1. Water boils at 212 degrees Fahrenheit.

2. A bad enough hurricane will snap a suspension bridge right in half.

So what I'm wondering is, does that mean fact three is, Every person has their breaking point? And if that's true, where's mine?

I guess it's obvious by now that I'm not exactly fond of my status as scientific freak and government pawn. My whole child-hood was spent being trained, not raised, by my dad, the big hero who disappeared the minute my mom was killed. I was left behind with ridiculously overdeveloped muscles, an excess of useless "knowledge," and about a billion questions that nobody can answer.

The only time I use my uncanny knack for foreign languages is when I'm ordering an *empanada* at San Loco.

I get passed around from family to family. People I love get killed left and right. I hook up with the love of my life, lose my virginity to him, and he almost gets his head splattered across the sidewalk as a direct result. Then my father shows up—oh, no, wait! Now I've got two identical guys claiming to be my dad, each warning me about the other. And with all this knowledge, with all these instincts, with all the roundhouse kicks and karate chops in the world, I can't figure out what the real deal is.

Here's the bitch of it: When I'm fighting, I know where I stand. A kick delivered to a solar plexus has a different effect from one aimed at the knee or, my personal favorite, the crotch. Thanks to my absent fear gene, I feel steely cool, in control, and smooth.

The minute the fight is over and I recover from the strain, nothing makes sense anymore. I try to sleep at night, and questions scuttle around in my brain like water bugs in a subway tunnel. My mom is dead, my dad is missing, and I have to pretend to hate my boyfriend (that is, if he even *is* my boyfriend) just to save his frigging life. I hate this. I absolutely hate the crap I deal with on a daily basis.

It reminds me of this scene in *Moby Dick*. This guy is left behind in a little boat while his whaling ship takes off without him. He watches the ship disappear and he's left for three days out there, just him, the water, the sky, and an unbroken horizon. He goes completely crazy from the loneliness.

That's how I feel. Inside, there's just flat, brackish water as far as the eye can see, and there's not a ship in sight to pick me up and show me where to go next.

Something's got to give or I swear, I'll reach my boiling point, I'll snap, and anything I say will be lunchtime fodder for the head shrink at your friendly neighborhood insane asylum.

With that, he
locked lips
with her,
and Heather
felt **overactive**
like
she **hormones**
was drinking
turbocharged
Gatorade.

GAIA STEPPED OUT OF THE DANK

De Facto subway station and into an equally dank, overcast morning just typical for late March on the East Coast. She strode down-town on Lexington, the sidewalk cluttered with strollers, nannies, and purebred dogs. It was early in the morning, but they were already out in full force: the perfect people, spending wads of money on Lexus strollers and canine cologne.

Downtown, where Gaia used to live, the buildings were smaller and the people a little more on the ball. Within blocks of her brownstone were immigrant neighborhoods whose streets brimmed with personality. Exotic smells drifted out of shops whose signs were handwritten in different languages. Chinatown. Little Italy. Up here, everything looked as bland and generic as a J. Crew catalog, and Gaia had given it her own name: Little Connecticut.

She had a job to do this morning, and she wasn't looking forward to it. When she'd first gotten parked in the superfancy digs of Natasha and her daughter, Tatiana, she'd been pretty peeved. Her dad had a habit of ditching her in the well-appointed apartments of his friends while he indulged his five-year-old habit of totally ignoring her existence. But what had started out as annoyance at the two Russian women's insistence on interfering with her life had become decidedly more sinister.

It was bad enough Russkie the Younger (that

would be Tatiana) had her eye on Gaia's would-be boyfriend, Ed. Russkie the Elder (the lovely Natasha, for those of you playing along at home) was not only digging her enameled nails into Tom Moore's heart, she was betraying his every stupid, lovesick move to Tom's evil twin brother, Loki.

Gaia didn't want to believe it. She would have much preferred to be one of the world's trusting idiots, a blissful moron convinced of the basic goodness of humanity. But there was optimism, and then there was reality. Gaia had learned, once and for all, not to hope for the best when the worst was, invariably, about to smack her upside the head.

The only thing she could do now was confront Natasha and get her the hell away from her dad.

Of course, there was the nagging question of why she owed Tom anything. Thanks to Oliver's surprise visit to the apartment the night before, Gaia wasn't even sure that he was her actual dad. Oliver, otherwise known as Loki, was his identical twin, and he claimed to be Gaia's dad, too, and neither one had done much of a job of convincing her.

Then again, Gaia had to admit, the letters Tom had given her—sheaves and sheaves of paper dating back to when she was twelve, detailing how much he loved her, missed her, and hated to have to leave her, neatly typed and hand signed every single day that they hadn't been together—were pretty convincing evidence that he, at least, gave a crap where she woke up and who she hung out with, even if he had disappeared for most of her adolescence. The letters were way corny with emotion. Not to mention that other epistolary collection—the letters from Tom to that snake Natasha, detailing his hopes for his daughter, filled with such longing, it hurt to think about them. So Gaia had to figure that even if he wasn't her biological father, he at least had a stake in her well-being—despite the fact that it was Oliver who appeared, like magic, whenever she most needed him.

She stepped into the ornate foyer of the building, her sneakers squeaking on the marble floor, and hit the elevator button. She studied her reflection in the thin strip of brass behind the button. High forehead, dirty blond hair hanging to her waist, and an angry set to her jaw. This was the face that Tom thought about every day? Nothing like the so-called normal girls at the Village School. Gaia wasn't convinced—but she wasn't about to be taken for a ride by Natasha.

If getting to the bottom of the situation meant, de facto, helping her "father," then so be it.

IT WAS AMAZING, TOM MOORE MUSED,

Regular Guy

that you could be sur- rounded by so much

physical beauty and still be dealing with ugly, menacing danger. He stepped out on the terrace of his hotel room, scanning the white beach and turquoise water for any sign of spies or hit men but saw only frolicking tourists, and hotel employees, dressed in spanking-white tunics, carrying trays of umbrella-topped drinks and piles of fluffy white towels. For a moment he allowed himself to relax as Natasha came up behind him and wound her arms around his torso, caressing his chest as she kissed the very center of his back. Their first night together had been filled with more passion than he'd felt since Katia's death, followed by the first full night's sleep he'd had since then, too.

"You're up early," he said.

"Not as early as you," she responded in her lilting Russian accent, running her fingernails up his chest.

"I suppose I have a touch of jet lag from my trip down from New York," she added, pouring coffee from the tall silver decanter that room service had placed outside their door. "Anyway, we have work to do," she said with a sigh.

Tom just gazed out the window.

"You are thinking about Gaia?" Natasha asked.

"She's so far away," Tom said, stepping inside, leaving the sliding doors wide open so that the humid tropical air filled the room. He picked up the delicate coffee cup in one hand and slugged down the rich black liquid. "I don't like being where I can't rush in if something happens to her."

"But you're almost never near enough to her—physically, I mean—to do that," Natasha pointed out as she stirred two lumps of sugar into her coffee and broke a biscotti in half. "It must be torment. I don't even like being away from Tatiana for a weekend."

"It's been like having an arm cut off," Tom agreed. "If I can just take care of Loki, I'll be able to be her father again—I won't have to worry that just by being near her, I'm putting her life in danger."

"Then that's what we'll do," Natasha said, with such conviction Tom believed they'd really do it this time.

"At least I know we're close," he said. "Somehow that takes the edge off the stress. I don't remember when I've ever felt so. . ."

"Carefree?"

"Not exactly. But something approaching it." He put down his coffee and stroked his finger softly along the delicate flesh that peeked from the top of Natasha's bathrobe.

Tom's Blackberry beeped. He jumped and broke away to see what the minicomputer had to say to him. "What is it?" Natasha asked, seeing a shadow cross his face.

"There's a delay," he answered her. "The operative we're supposed to track isn't going to be here for another day."

Tom felt the familiar clutch in his gut, telling him he could do nothing but lay low till someone, somewhere, did their job. Normally he hated downtime; action quieted the noise in his head. But this time? This time the agony of impatience was almost immediately replaced by relief—and even joy.

In the five years since his wife's murder, Tom had never allowed himself to get close to anyone. Sure, he had his colleagues at the Agency. And he could always depend on George Niven to give him honest, fatherly counsel when he needed it. But since he had been forced to distance himself from his daughter, it seemed that his heart, unable to shower its love on the one he most wanted to be with, had just hardened into a dull lump in his chest.

But now? Something had changed. He didn't know if it was just the passage of time, or Natasha's passing resemblance to Katia, or something else—like true love—but he was feeling his heart begin to beat again, and he began to actually believe there might be an end to these years of constant struggle.

Yes. Maybe this wasn't a waste of a day. Maybe his work here in the Cayman Islands wasn't the only thing he had to think about. Maybe for once he could stop being Tom Moore, government agent, and just for a little while become **Tom Moore**, regular guy.

HEATHER WAS GIDDY ENOUGH TO

Über-
Gwyneth

actually be bouncing as she walked into the Starbucks near school. It was time to meet Josh, and every nerve ending in her body was alert with anticipation.

He had already ordered up a grande for her, remembering the dash of cinnamon and extra foam. She loved how attentive he was. Suddenly being slighted by Sam and Ed in favor of Gaia didn't matter—Josh was more intriguing than either of them had been, and he was interested only in her.

"Good morning," she said, taking the foamy drink from his hand and sticking her cheek out for him to kiss.

"Same to you, gorgeous," he answered, nuzzling her hair so that she shivered with the delicious warmth of it. "And what's on the schedule for this hot student body?"

"I predict a pop quiz on T. S. Eliot in my advanced

11

English class," she said. "We're reading *The Waste Land.*"

"Oh, yeah—'April is the cruelest month' and all that?" Josh asked, his cheeks dimpling in the most adorable way as he flashed his gorgeous grin. "I remember getting lost in that poem. Parts of it are so sad. You're lucky to be reading it for the first time."

"Oh, I read it in seventh grade," Heather revealed, shaking her head. "It's brilliant. And 'The Love Song of J. Alfred Prufrock,' too. 'In the room the women come and go, talking of Michelangelo. . . .'"

"Yeah, I think I overheard those women when I took a shortcut through Bergdorf's." Josh laughed.

"Ugh, don't remind me," Heather said. His joke hit home for Heather. Her own "friends" were like cardboard cutouts, yapping about paraffin manicures, Brazilian bikini waxes, and parties in the Hamptons. And somehow she was their queen. Which meant she had to pretend to be as vapid as they were just to survive in their presence.

She looked at Josh, gazing deeply into his eyes. It was so clear to her that he really cared about her. That was why he was going to help her. Help her outdo Gaia once and for all.

"So I've been thinking," she said, leaning forward conspiratorially. "About that little visit we made? To your friend's. . . apartment the other day?"

"Oh, yeah," Josh said, pulling back from her a bit. "I'm sorry if that freaked you out. I wouldn't be surprised if you never wanted to talk about it again. Unless. . ."

"Unless what?" Heather asked.

"Well." Josh let out a sigh as he seemed to collect his thoughts. "I just—I feel like—ugh, this sounds so stupid."

"No, go on," Heather encouraged him.

"I feel like there's a connection between us," Josh said. "There's something about you that I really respond to, and I just—I really like being around you, you know?"

Heather's heart pounded. "I, uh—yes, I do know," she said, trying with every fiber of her being not to sound like an immature dork.

"And I think what I'm feeling from you is just, like, this energy, this spirit, that sets you apart from other girls. And I feel like if you could magnify that energy. . ." He looked at her, his blue eyes wide with possibility. "I just think you'd be unstoppable. I think you'd be a bright, shiny creature that would make people gasp with awe."

"I. . . oh!" Heather had no idea what to say. She couldn't believe Josh saw that part of her, the part she never showed anyone.

"But hey. This is your decision, you know? Anyway, I interrupted you. Were you going to ask me something about it?"

"I was," Heather said. Then she paused. Josh made it sound so enticing—like this experiment would change her life and turn her into one of those charmed creatures for whom everything seems to go right and over whom everyone seems to flip. Like some sort of *über*-Gwyneth.

"I just wish I had a little more information—like it'd be nice to know exactly what it is that they're giving me," she said. "And whether there's some sort of release I'll have to sign? How do I know they're not going to implant a homing device in my skull? Little things like that."

"Ah. Shoot." Josh looked disappointed. It felt like the sun had just gone behind a cloud; Heather couldn't stand to see his face fall like that.

"I'm not saying no!" she insisted. "I just have a few questions."

"Oh, gorgeous," Josh said, putting his arms around her and dragging both Heather and her chair into the warm place where she was totally surrounded by his presence. "You don't have to do anything. . . ."

"I'm not saying no," she repeated.

"Yeah. But you're second guessing yourself," he said, brushing a stray hair off her cheek. "That kind of thinking is for the cookie-cutter people, the ones who inspect every opportunity while feeling too terrified to ever actually act."

Heather sighed, running her fingers along the

highly toned bicep that was draped across her chest. "You're making it all sound so tempting," she said. "I just want to think it over some more. Is that all right?" She looked up, meeting his eyes and hoping not to see that awful disappointment again.

He sighed, too. It wasn't quite disappointment. Maybe more like hope. "I wish you'd do it," he said. "I want the best for you. I want everyone to see what I see in you."

With that, he locked lips with her, and Heather felt like she was drinking turbocharged Gatorade.

"I'll keep taking these," she promised, opening her bag so he could see the prescription bottle. "That way I'll be ready at a moment's notice when it's time to do it. All right?"

"That's totally cool," Josh said. "Think it over. I know you'll make the right decision, whatever it is."

Heather relaxed and nestled into his muscular warmth. As she sat breathing in his musky scent, her mind wandered into a reverie: Her and Gaia facing off, Gaia focused and determined until Heather began fighting back with amazing speed. Then she saw Gaia's face fall apart like a puzzle, confused and startled by Heather's new grace, speed, and bravery. Heather finished her off with a kick to the gut, and Gaia fell. In her daydream Heather turned to see Josh, who nodded, took her by the hand, and drew her in for a passionate smooch. Heather shivered as a delicious thrill ran through her.

"Cold?" Josh asked, rubbing her arm.

"Stone-cold," Heather answered with a grin.

ED LAY ON HIS BACK ON A TABLE, his legs pumping at a beeping machine. He was trying to concentrate on making his legs work on the weird StairMaster thing, but mostly he was trying to ignore the fact that a woman with the body of a Playboy Playmate was kneading the muscles of his thighs. This was like the beginning of a really bad late night Showtime movie.

Maxim-Level Hotness

"So, uh. . . where's Brian again?"

"He's out in San Francisco for the next few weeks," said Lydia, his substitute physical therapist. "Taking an advanced seminar in dynamic massage. You're stuck with me today."

Stuck? Lydia was hot. Which in any other setting would be a fine way for Ed to take his mind off his confusion over Gaia and Tatiana. But in this case, it was cause for distraction. Ed tried to think about baseball.

"Feel the burn?" Lydia asked.

16

"Sheee-yeah," Ed grumbled.

"All right. We have to talk." Thankfully, Lydia took her hand off Ed's upper leg and crossed her arms. She glared at Ed, and he wondered if his overactive hormones were somehow showing. *Hey, I'm just a healthy, red-blooded American,* he thought.

"Do you want to tell me why you're still on those crutches when you clearly don't need them anymore?"

What?

"Uh, hello, Earth to medical professional," Ed said, rolling his eyes. "I was in a massive skateboarding accident? Big hill, no brakes, Ed meets gravel? Two years in a wheelchair? Is any of this ringing a bell?"

Lydia laughed and turned to face him. "Yeah. But that's all in the past now. You've progressed a lot further than you're willing to admit, but you won't take that first step."

Ed stared at her, flabbergasted.

"I see this a lot," Lydia said. "The heart wants to get up and walk out of the chair, but the mind is still scared. Ed, there's nothing to be scared of. You can walk without your crutches, and if you let yourself, you can move on from your accident and all the pain it brought you."

Ed blinked. "Is that true? Why didn't Brian tell me?"

"He was probably just being soft on you," Lydia said. "Hoping you'd figure it out on your own. But that's not my MO. If you don't try walking before I see you next time—take a break from the crutches—I'm going to recommend that you get cut off from any more physical therapy."

A break? Ed wanted to toss the stupid crutches into a vat of sulfuric acid. But did Lydia know what she was talking about?

"How come you're so sure?" Ed asked. It seemed too easy, like the end of an episode of "Touched by an Angel." He stared at her. "How do I know I can do it?"

"You *don't* know you can do it," Lydia told him. "That's the problem. But I do." She sighed, giving a decidedly unnurturing and rough massage to his calves. What this woman had in *Maxim*-level hotness, she sure was missing in bedside manner.

Ed stared at the ceiling. He couldn't ask Lydia any more questions. He knew he sounded like a total baby. But even if what she was saying was true, he didn't have the slightest idea what to do next.

Her tough-love treatment was suddenly softened by a couple of words of advice. "All right," she finally told him. "Here's the five-step plan. First, you get out of this environment. I know you've been working on the parallel bars, but that's the last thing I would recommend for a young guy like you. The sight of all those old geezers getting over their strokes is messing with your head. You need to try this somewhere that's home to you—where you used to be able to walk."

"Got it," Ed said. "Nix the hospital setting."

"You're smarter than you look," Lydia told him. "Now, the second thing is, don't re-create the hospital in your home. Most people will strategically place large items of furniture all over the place, figuring they can lurch from the kitchen table to the counter and pretend that's walking. It's not."

"No?"

"Not even a little." Lydia looked down at him. "When my little brother was learning to walk, he always had to have something in his hand—didn't matter whether it was connected to anything or not. If he was holding a block, a piece of blanket, even a carrot, he could waddle around, no problem. But if you took away whatever was in his hand, he thumped to the ground like his butt was a magnet and the floor was made of steel."

"I'll bet you took that little hunk of blanket away from him every chance you could," Ed wagered.

"Yep. I figured he'd be better off." Lydia shrugged. "Call it early training."

You scare me, Ed thought. "So what's three?"

"Step three—fix your eyes on something across the room," Lydia said. "Focus on it so it's all you see. Never look down. Pretend the floor isn't there. Just fixate on getting to that point on the wall, and you'll make it."

"Uh-huh." It sounded like a good idea. Then again,

eating boogers had sounded like a good idea when he was five.

"Number four is you have to just see your legs doing their work in your head. Forget trying to force them and straining to work each muscle," Lydia said. "You never did that before you lost the use of your legs. Just see them walking in your mind, like you're watching a movie, and it'll jog their muscle memory."

"Get it? Jog," Ed cracked before he could stop himself. He wanted so desperately to charm her, he was willing to go with his weakest material. Lydia didn't even pretend to smile.

"And five," she said. "Leap."

"Leap? I can't walk first?"

"Leap of faith," she told him. "Stop thinking so much and just do it."

Ed lay quietly, running through the five-step plan in his head. "Okay," he said. "I'll try it."

"Jedi warrior no try," Lydia told him. "Jedi warrior do."

Finally, an opening for a decent comeback—"Thank you, Yoda. But I can't make any promises."

Still nothing. She didn't even skip a beat. It was as if she had blocked all her joke receptors. "So don't. It's no skin off my nose if you stay on those crutches the rest of your life. It's yourself you should be making the promise to."

20

Okay, he thought. *Ed, I promise I'll. . . walk.* Even inside his head, he sounded like a total doofus.

SO THIS IS AMERICA, TATIANA THOUGHT

Nuclear Strike

as she sat alone in her giant, empty apartment. No mother, no friends, a boy who kissed her but still loved someone else, and no parties to take her mind off her problems. If this was the great USA, she'd just as soon get back on the airplane and make the thirteen-hour flight back home. At least there she had a life.

She sighed, wandered into the kitchen, and opened the refrigerator. This country. *What kind of people name a food "La Yogurt"?* Did they think they were going to fool anyone into thinking the French sat around eating strawberry-banana goo? Realizing she wasn't hungry, she slammed the door shut and continued her circuit of the apartment.

Maybe she could get a dog to keep her company. But that would never work. People picked up their dogs' droppings in this city. She sighed again and flicked on the radio in the living room, letting the ambient music of the dance-mix deejay fill the room. Twirling the volume dial up high, she noticed that her fingernails looked pathetically raggedy.

"You are going down the tubes," she scolded herself. Then she inspected her hands closely. Dry skin, and about a centimeter of cuticle showing.

Tatiana knew her mother had just gotten a fancy nail kit. She'd probably be annoyed at her for breaking it in, but that was her problem. If she was going to desert her daughter like this, she deserved to lose an emery board or two.

Tatiana entered her mother's ornate, marble bathroom and looked around. The bathrobe hanging behind the door made her heart lurch—she missed Natasha horribly and didn't understand why these "translating emergencies" and special projects always called her away. Wasn't there anyone else who could do the job for the UN? Someone who didn't have a daughter? Tatiana opened the twin doors of the vanity under the sink and began digging through the bottles, boxes, and tubes piled up underneath.

"Mother, you're single-handedly keeping Sephora in business," she grumbled. "Ah!" she yelped, finally reaching a zippered black pouch.

She sat on the cool tiles and unzipped the patent leather, expecting nothing more than a buffer and some scissors. But something fluttered out and landed on the frilly yellow rug.

Tatiana picked it up and felt a wave of heat radiate from her heart. What was the English word for this feeling?

"Oh, gross," she said aloud.

It was a greeting card. With hearts and angels and flowers. Inside—Tatiana couldn't help opening it—was a note scrawled in masculine handwriting.

Natasha, I can't wait until you join me in the islands. The few days we'll be separated will be torture. Thank you for coming into my life. Tom.

Gross? This was worse than gross. It made her want to vomit.

She was used to Natasha dating. That was normal. And anyway, nobody ever really touched her mother, not in her heart. But this sentimental missive—from Gaia's father—was more than she could bear.

Perhaps she was misinterpreting the note. She read it a second time. And a third. She turned it upside down and sideways, but there was nothing to misinterpret—Tom had it bad for her mother.

So what did this mean for Tatiana? In a wildest, worst-case scenario, it meant Gaia wasn't going to be just a temporary irritation. As long as their parents were together, Tatiana and Gaia would be forced to hang around together, too. Any vacation she took—even back home to Russia, to finally see her family and friends again—would include the two of them, too.

Thirteen hours on a plane with Gaia? *Ach.*

Or maybe the two of them would only vacation alone—as they were apparently doing right now, Tatiana realized with a rush of fury. Last minute emergency, indeed: Natasha had lied to her—lied to her own daughter's face—and made her worry, when all the time she was carousing on a tropical island with the father of the worst girl in the entire world.

Argh! Tatiana wanted to rip the card in two. She was poised to do just that when an even more horrible thought produced an image that flashed across her consciousness with all the power and brightness of a nuclear strike: *What if they get married?*

Tatiana imagined the wedding: her mother in ivory lace, Tom in a dark suit, herself in an elegant blue Shelli Segal dress. . . and Gaia in combat boots and a flannel shirt.

Ugh! Gaia as a stepsister!

Tatiana was about to rip the note in two, knowing her mother would kill her and just not caring, when she froze. *What was. . .*

The music in the living room kept up its steady pounding. But there was some other noise, too. Something like a window thumping closed after having been thumped open?

For a moment she thought her mother was home and would walk in and see all her toiletries on the floor and Tatiana in the middle of them, with the evidence of her snooping right there in her hands. That gave her a moment of high-level anxiety. Then she realized that if her mother had come in the front door, she would have heard the alarm activate. If someone was in the apartment, he had come in through a window. Attempting to arrive undetected.

A burglar, perhaps. Or worse. . .

She swallowed hard and raced down to the living room, feeling icy cold with fear. She felt a rush of relief as she saw the windows were all safely shut.

Then she saw it.

The vase from the windowsill.

Someone had kicked it to the floor. . . on their way in through the window.

Sure enough, the window was completely unlocked. Tatiana touched it with trembling fingers, then turned her back to it, flattening herself against the glass as she realized:

She might have started out the evening alone in this apartment.

But someone was in here with her now.

What is it that Humphrey
Bogart says in *Casablanca*? "Of
all the gin joints in all the
world, why'd she have to walk
into mine?"

That's how I feel about
Heather. Of all the overprivi-
leged teenage girls in all the
private high schools in this
city, why did Loki have to pick
her to be his victim?

I know I'm supposed to do my
job without emotion. I'm a hired
gun, and I should have no more
conscience than that lead-filled
hunk of metal.

But Heather? I can't see this
happening to her.

Loki told me to woo her into
participating in his scheme, and I
did—at first. But as I get to know
this girl better, my empty, seduc-
tive words actually begin to fill
with meaning. I wasn't lying when
I told her she had something in
her that others don't. She's not
like those friends of hers.
There's something dark inside her,

some part of her that waffles back
and forth between giving in to the
easy, shallow way out—and really
living her life on a deeper level.

I think if she were left alone
and given time, she'd turn into
an amazing woman.

I think she's more beautiful
than she'll ever realize.

I think she's got the kind of
mind that makes her endlessly
fascinating.

I think I'm falling in love
with her.

Jesus. If Loki ever found out
what was going on inside my heart
right now, I wouldn't just get
fired. I'd be dead meat. Total
and complete worm food.

But I can't help it. Heather's
an amazing girl, and I'm not
going to let him get to her. I'll
stop trying to convince her to be
part of this experiment; I'll
keep her away from him, maybe get
her out of town for a while, convince him that she's all wrong
for his master plan.

The truth is, I don't know

what the real effect of this experiment will be—nobody does. She's the first human subject. He could shoot her up and her eyeballs could explode or her bones could melt or something.

I watched him try it out on an entire petting zoo full of fluffy creatures, with varying levels of success.

I think if she'd seen what happened to the monkey, she wouldn't be so eager to try this out.

But let's say the injection works—physically. Let's say this phobosan stuff enters her bloodstream, changing her DNA so that she has no fear. And her head doesn't fly off in the process. She's totally unprepared for a new life.

Not to sound all Oprah, but she's totally ill equipped to face this brave new Heather. It's like putting her behind the wheel of a Mack truck and expecting her to drive it cross-country.

And here's the pathetic part: I'm worried how she'll feel about me. I know how I feel about her—I know nothing could shake the love I feel. I know I feel better, more like myself, when she's around, plain and simple. She seems to be into me, but what if that's just another manifestation of her fear? Just like her friends, her clothes, and all of her other status symbols. What if I'm just a security blanket? Then she won't need me after she gets the injection.

I've just developed a conscience, and its first order of business is to keep Heather safe.

Stroll. *Amble, traipse,*
step out. Stride, pace, hoof it.
Or if you're feeling down,
trudge. Plod, shamble, shuffle.
Waddle. Slink. Tiptoe.

I think my personal favorite
is *saunter.* I don't think people
really saunter anymore. Maybe I
should revive the lost art of
sauntering.

However you decide to say it—
whatever word you pull out of the
thesaurus—apparently Ed Fargo *can*
walk if he wants to. I can put my
feet to the pavement, sans
crutches, and perambulate from
West Fourth Street to Battery
Park if I so choose. And the only
reason I haven't done it so far?

Women.

Most specifically two women,
the lovely and troubled Gaia and
the lovely and foreign Tatiana.
While one's been running away,
the other's been chasing me down,
and I've been so busy being stuck
in the middle, I forgot about
myself.

Well, that's over with.

When I kissed Tatiana, it was like—I mean, I'm a guy. It was great! She's pretty, she thinks I'm a rock star, and she's fun to be with. I should have made out with her for hours and forgotten all about Gaia and her random acts of cruelty.

Except I can't forget Gaia. From the moment I first saw her— from the four-wheeled prison I sat in for two years—I just adored that scowling, crabby face. I fell for her like a sack of cement. Becoming her best friend was a welcome challenge, and she's the most important person in my life. Full of energy and completely mysterious.

And I had her. I had her right there in my bed, I slept next to her in what seems now like some kind of enchanted subconscious fantasy somehow sprung to life, and in the space of time it took me to hobble downstairs to grab some chow, she vanished like Madonna's American accent.

That messed with my head. And much as I'd like to drown my sorrows in a pool of Tatiana, I've got other fish to fry.

It's time to take a break from the fairer sex and concentrate on these two useless bowling pins I'm supposed to be using as legs. Apparently I've been knocked off my feet. I've got to get myself up and running.

If he ever
met Gene
Simmons, he
was going
to kick his
glam-
rocking,
tongue-
wagging,
makeup-
wearing ass.

TATIANA WHEELED AROUND, HER

Unknown Quantity from Hell

heart pounding. Who was in here with her? She heard something knock in the next room. What was she supposed to do? If she kept silent, the intruder might take whatever he wanted and leave without knowing she was there. But if he found her—it was too horrible. She should start screaming now, and maybe someone would hear her before he found her. . . .

A weapon. She needed a weapon. Glad that she'd kicked off her shoes the minute she walked into the apartment, Tatiana slunk toward the kitchen, petrified that a `creaking floorboard` would give her away. Once there, she silently drew the chopping knife out of the block and wondered what to do next.

Am I really supposed to stab somebody? she wondered. *What if he gets the knife from me?*

She hastily replaced the cold steel blade on the counter and jumped as she heard footsteps coming toward the back of the apartment. She slipped out of the room, flattening herself into the alcove that led to the back door, wondering if she could get it unlocked and open without tipping off the intruder. Then she heard the footsteps thumping away again. Tatiana peeked out and saw a box of Fig Newtons open on the counter.

Hungry robbers? Maybe they were doing so many drugs, they had the crunchies, or whatever Americans call those marijuana-induced cravings, and needed to eat before emptying the house of electronics?

Tatiana knew she had to get out of the apartment, but there was so much crap in front of the back door— endless pairs of her mother's boots, cardboard boxes full of her files—that there was no way she was going to get out this way. She slipped silently into the hallway, checking to make sure it was empty, and darted into the bathroom, getting that much closer to the front door.

She would run out and start screaming immediately. She would bang on all the doors, and someone would have to hear her. If not, she would take the stairs down and yell for the doorman. Anything was better than remaining in here with the unknown quantity from hell.

She stood, taut with tension, waiting to see if another noise would let her know where the intruder was. What she heard sent a chill through her gut: the stereo in the living room being switched off with a loud click.

In the silence, she knew any footfall would be heard immediately. But she had to take a chance. Every nerve screaming, Tatiana made a break for the door.

Her face met flesh as she ran smack into a human form, bouncing backward at the sheer shock of it. All her tension erupted, and she let out a full-throated roar of terror that surprised even her.

"Chill out, Tatiana. It's just me."

Gaia. Gaia?

"Gaia!" Tatiana breathed, barely able to get the name out over the pounding of her heart. "What in the world are you doing? Did you come in through the window?"

"Yeah. So?" Gaia shrugged as if she hadn't just scared the living daylights out of her roommate.

"Why?" Tatiana asked, following Gaia's nonchalant form back into the kitchen, where she opened the refrigerator and started making a cream-cheese-and-jelly sandwich.

"I didn't feel like running into you," Gaia said. "I knew you'd start in with a million nagging questions. I was just trying to have a little privacy."

"And you do this by coming in like a cat stealer?" Tatiana asked.

"I think you mean a cat burglar," Gaia said, rolling her eyes.

That was all Tatiana needed. Rage exploded through her body, and she took the sandwich out of Gaia's hands and threw it on the floor.

"Don't you dare correct me!" she screamed, slamming

a hand on the counter. "You frightened me terribly, and you can't even say you're sorry. You're rude, and you're inconsiderate, and I wish you did not live in my house!"

Gaia stared at her, mouth open in disbelief.

"Would you chill out?" she said. "It's no big deal."

"It *is* a big deal," Tatiana told her. "If my mother were here, I would tell her that I want you to leave."

"Your mother." Gaia moaned, rolling her eyes again. "Yeah, there's an authority figure I'd be comfortable with."

"What do you mean?" Tatiana snapped. "You are going to insult my mother?"

Gaia seemed to be about to speak, but she stopped. "No. I wasn't going to say anything."

"Good. Because if I had to have you permanently in my life, I'd. . ."

Now it was Tatiana's turn to hold back. She wasn't going to give Gaia any ammunition to hurt her with. If Gaia didn't know their parents were romantically involved, Tatiana wasn't going to tell her.

"I have to live with you, I suppose," Tatiana said. "So until my mother returns from her trip, why don't you move into the living room? You and I can avoid each other more easily that way. We don't even have to meet in the kitchen if we stick to a schedule."

"Fine. I hate sharing a room," Gaia said. "I don't need you all up in my business." She picked up her sandwich from the floor, brushed it off, and took a bite, dribbling crumbs on the tiled floor. Then she strolled out of the kitchen and toward their bedroom, grabbing her duffel bag out of the front-hall closet on her way.

"I don't want to be inside of your business, anyway!" Tatiana called after her. "Damn!" she said, then let loose a torrent of curses in Russian. Gaia spoke about a bazillion languages. She'd probably get the gist.

I'm not going to sit here and moan about my life. I made a choice as a young man, and I knew my existence would never truly be my own after that. But when I step back and look at it, I have to be impressed with the chaos I've survived.

At least I've survived. I can't say the same for a lot of people I loved.

When Katia told me Gaia was coming, I wasn't fully prepared to be a father. I was wrapped up in my wife and didn't want to share her with anyone. But once Gaia was born, I was struck to the core. My God, this soft little creature looked to me and Katia for everything. We became a culture of three, a little tribe that stood outside the regular world and created our own society.

I had twelve years of near bliss. Isn't that more than most people get?

And then it was taken away. And I don't know if Albert

TOM

Tennyson was right when he said that it's better to have loved and lost than never to have loved at all. Because the absence of that warmth has been torture.

Natasha has touched me in a way that no one has been able to since Katia's death. Natasha's giving me a taste of that bliss and, dare I think it, promising me the potential to live that way again. I fought her. I'll admit it. I didn't want to fall in love again. But this hitch in our plans—this day of complete idleness in the middle of an operation—is sealing the deal on my feelings for her.

For a full twenty-four hours I have nothing to do but drink her in.

I'm not a great believer in fate, but whatever the cause of our delay, it has had the result of pushing us together, when we'd never have found the time otherwise. And it seems like it's just meant to be.

Listen to me. I sound like a stupid kid. If I were my superior, I'd fire me in a second.

Hello, Ed! Are you out there? If I yell out my window, will you be standing downstairs like some kind of twenty-first century Romeo? Or will I just attract a collection of curious New Yorkers who will glare at me and then tell me to "shaddap"?

How about if I call to you with my mind? I'll close my eyes and think, *Ed Fargo, Ed Fargo, Ed Fargo,* and that will open up a metaphysical channel to your heart. I'll make a mental QuickTime movie of our kiss and e-mail it to your brain. Then perhaps you will remember the Russian girl you spent so much time with.

All right, Tatiana. Get ahold of yourself. It has only been one day since the kiss—not even a full twenty-four hours. The boy has not called you, but he might be busy and distracted. Or maybe he is waiting on purpose so he doesn't seem too overeager.

Oh, but I hate this waiting on purpose.

I know I'm overanxious because
Gaia has put me in a state of
extreme tension, but I also
really like this boy, Ed. I've
been horribly lonely since I came
here from Russia, and he was the
first person to show me around
and introduce me to this strange,
dirty city. I mean, pepperoni
pizza—who knew there was such a
thing?

I really like Ed. I want him
to call me.

Just my luck I have to share a
home with the girl he loves. Who
hates me for no reason, who uses
up the good intentions that my
mother has for her, and who comes
in the window at all hours when
there is a perfectly good door
for her to use. Gaia. Gaia the
infinitely infuriating.

Okay. If he doesn't call in
one half hour, I will send him an
e-mail. Just a friendly e-mail.
An electronic message from my
heart to his, disguised as an
innocent hello. Of course, how to
make this sound so innocent is

difficult. If only I could write to him in Russian! I'd know just how to do it so that I didn't sound anxious or needy. Too bad Ed Fargo is about as Russian as a Chicken McNugget.

A cute, friendly, heartbreaking Chicken McNugget.

To: shred@alloymail.com
From: russkiegirl@alloymail.com

Ed,

So this is what kissing is like in America! I have to admit, it was as delicious as the pizza you introduced me to. So what happens next?

I do not expect you to have an answer for me. I know you are feeling conflicted. You still have feelings for Gaia.

You have to work this out for yourself, but I just want to say this: I am not conflicted, and I would never be cold to you the way she is. If you sit back and think about this, I know you'll eventually see the truth.

Just don't make me wait too long.

                                        Tatiana

[DELETED]

ED WENT STRAIGHT HOME TO TEST

Gene's Tongue

out Lydia's five-step plan. First period would just have to wait.

He was out of the hospital, away from the geezers, in the place where he felt most comfortable. In fact, in the very apartment where he'd learned to walk in the first place. He was alone, too. And there was nothing here to impede his progress across the floor. Except his own stupid brain.

He sat on his bed, the crutches tucked neatly underneath so he couldn't see them and feel tempted to use them. His armpits felt sort of cold and lonely without them. But they were going to have to get used to that—at least, he hoped they would.

Across the room, tacked to the wall with Scotch tape, was a vintage Kiss poster, from the early days of their reign as the most dangerous band on the planet—back when they still had some credibility. Paul Stanley gazed at the camera with a tight-lipped pout, the black star over his left eye betraying a hint of shine. At his right stood Gene Simmons, the cheesiest rocker on the planet, his extra-long tongue stuck out so far, it touched his chin.

Ed wasn't really a member of the Kiss army. He was more like, say, a member of the Kiss National Guard or maybe the Kiss ROTC. Their music was stupid, but something about its kitsch factor made him happy. Plus they made his sister break out in hives at their grossness. That was a bonus.

Hence the poster on his wall. He hadn't even noticed it in months, really, but right now, it was the most obvious object for him to use as a focal point.

But where should he concentrate his attention?

He decided on Gene's tongue rather than Paul's star, just because Paul was such a favorite of the ladies, which made him way less cool in Ed's eyes.

So here he was in his room, with nothing to grab onto between his bed and Gene's tongue. Now all he had to do was stand up, visualize his legs moving, and take a leap of faith.

This was going to be easy. He tried a mental practice run before he stood up. Pictured his legs, skinnier now than they used to be but with a good amount of muscle built up from the physical therapy. On his feet were thick white socks and his oldest, comfiest pair of blue Chuck Taylor high-tops. He saw them stand and, without hesitation, walk across the room. Step after step, they covered the eight feet in no time flat. At first his imaginary movie looked kind of jerky, like it was shot from a flip book. After he tried it a few more times, the playback appeared in brightly saturated Technicolor. A little more practice and it took on the hiccupping cast of streaming video; an ounce more concentration and Ed was watching, in the amphitheater of his mind, the clear, definitive, ultimate-edition, director's-cut DVD of himself walking across the room, complete with alternate sound track and commentary. He was truly Xbox ready.

He stood, rewound the mental movie to the starting point, zeroed in on Gene's tongue, and took a leap of faith.

He saw the tongue; he felt his legs move; he took a step and. . .

Flopped like a flounder on the floor.

For a moment he was totally stunned. He actually thought he had made it across the room and was nose to nose with Ace Frehley. Slowly he realized he was actually face-to-face with a particularly rank patch of carpet.

First he became aware of a burning ache across his face. Then he felt a much more painful ache in his heart. He hadn't realized how much he had bought into Lydia's plan. He'd thought he prepared himself for failure, but he was devastated.

Five-step plan, my ass, he thought, wondering if his nose was broken. This wasn't as easy as it had sounded. Possibly Lydia was not only a bitch, she was a lunatic as well, all wrapped up in the body of Anna Kournikova.

He hadn't made it across the room. He didn't know

if he ever would. At that moment he only knew one thing.

If he ever met Gene Simmons, he was going to kick his glam-rocking, tongue-wagging, makeup-wearing ass.

GAIA FLOPPED ONTO THE COUCH and tried to picture how the room would look with her T-shirts, jeans, computer, and discs strewn about it. About the same as the rest of her life: a mess. She sighed, listening to Tatiana storming around the adjoining room, and threw her feet loudly onto the coffee table.

Goose Egg

She understood enough Russian and knew she ought to be outraged at the torrent of insults flooding from her roommate's mouth, but she just couldn't muster up the anger. After a moment it got quiet, and she heard Tatiana typing so hard, it was like she was beating up her computer's keyboard. Was she writing to Ed?

Ed. Gaia sank lower on the couch as she felt her guts melt, against her will, at the thought of the one peaceful, happy night she could remember ever having.

The sex itself had been nice, but sort of weird. The whole. . . physics of the act was bizarre, she had to admit. It would take some getting used to, though parts of it were already pretty excellent.

But getting used to it just wasn't in the cards. She and Ed had had one night—just the one—and if she cared about him at all, she had to cut him off cold. Despite her feelings for him—despite the total unraveling of every inch of resolve, and despite her total craving—now that she realized the depth of her feeling for him—to be near him all the time, wasn't it a cruel joke that she had to play ice princess and act like he meant absolutely nothing? Nada? Goose egg?

And wasn't he taking it well! The least he could do was be devastated, Gaia thought. But instead of mooning around looking like he felt as crappy as Gaia, he was off with Tatiana. There was no mistaking the attraction between the two of them. They were as chummy as—well, as Gaia and Ed used to be, hanging out together between classes and whatnot. It made Gaia want to barf.

"*Blech!*" she shouted at the ceiling.

The typing in the next room stopped. "Did you say something?" Tatiana called out.

"*No!*" Gaia replied. She had to get out of this apartment; it felt like a jail. And the sound of Tatiana endlessly typing long, epic-style Russian love notes to Gaia's one true love wasn't helping.

Gaia stood, yanked a sweater over her head, and slung her backpack over her shoulder. She'd spend the day roaming the city—check out the Met as long as she was up in this neighborhood, take in the sights, maybe bust up a mugging or two. One thing was for sure: She wasn't going to school today. She had way too much on her mind for that.

Forget it. This e-mail

sounds like something written
from Felicity or that Buffy who
slays the vampires. The only
vampire in my life is the one
who's sucking the life out of me
by living in my home and being a
big bitch. Maybe I should become
Tatiana the Bitch Slayer.

I'd really like to know why I
am being hated. Sure, she's angry
with me for hanging around with
Ed, but she's the one who's pushing him away. If she cares so
much, why doesn't she just stop?
Then she wouldn't feel the need
to constantly yell at me for no
reason, insult my mother, and
glare at me from the dark corner.

The craziest part of this is
that deep down, something inside
me wishes Gaia would be my
friend. How ridiculous!

It's just that she seems so—I
can say the word in Russian, but
I'd have to look it up in
English. *Self-possessed*, that's
what I was thinking of. She never

has a moment of doubt, never
questions if she is doing the
correct thing. I wish to be more
like that myself. And sometimes I
think, if she wasn't so angry,
she could be a lot of fun.

Something about her is just
attractive. Like a magnet. I can
see why Ed liked her, but she has
screwed that up, just like she
seems to screw everything else up
with her nasty attitude.

Forget it. Forget her. I'm
going to finish one more version
of this e-mail, then I've got to
get to school. Gaia might be willing to flunk out, but I'm much
more responsible than she is.

At least, I think I am. The
fact is, I don't know a thing
about her.

Memo

From: J

To: L

Subject is incredibly eager to move forward. However, recommend caution: she may be emotionally unstable. Perhaps another subject would be better?

Memo

From: L

To: J

I will worry about the subject's emotional state. You concern yourself with your job: drawing her in further and ensuring her participation. Reminder that time is of the essence. Subject must receive injection within forty-eight hours of phase 2. Otherwise she will be neutralized.

Memo

From: J

To: L

Understood. Humblest apologies for stepping out of line. Stepping up treatment now. Subject will be prepped for final experiment on schedule.

Sixes and nines
hopped on top of
each other in
carnal abandon,
and **decisions,**
the
ones **decisions**
and sevens were
having a complete
and total orgy
with the *y*'s.

SOME MORNINGS, ED WONDERED IF
high school was actually the
invention of evil scientists bent
on making adolescence even
more difficult than it was. Oh,
sure, on the surface it seemed
innocent enough. Practically perfect. Kids in cool clothes walked
from class to class, passing out
handmade posters demanding
that someone vote for someone
else for class president, just like on "Dawson's Creek."

Prom Queen Possessed

Or like the first ten minutes of
Nightmare on Elm Street.

How come everyone else seemed to have themselves totally pulled together? Did they really all
know where they were headed? Ed didn't even
understand where he'd been, let alone what he
should do next. He'd made a sort of decision to
avoid matters of the heart in favor of matters of his
legs, but he still wasn't sure this was going to work.
Was it possible to convince yourself you couldn't
walk? And could you really unconvince yourself of
that? He might look like a normal high school kid,
but he knew the truth: If anyone took an Ed Fargo
brain scan right now, they wouldn't see the wrinkled
lump of gray matter that was supposed to be there.
All they'd see was a sizzling fricassee

of what-do-I-do-now. Because that's all he was feeling.

Then again, he was better off than Heather, apparently. Ed's eyes widened as he realized that the faded version of Heather Gannis walking toward him down the hall was actually *the* Heather Gannis, the "House of Style" hostess of the entire Village School. She'd seemed pretty strung out the last time he'd seen her—dressed like a ten-year-old Barbie doll at a tag sale and pouring coffee down her throat like it was beer at a frat party—but he'd thought she'd just had one rough night. From the looks of her, things hadn't improved. She had dark circles under her eyes, her hair hung in unwashed sheets on either side of her face, and she was wearing jeans so old and raggedy, they looked like they were left over from the *first* Bush administration.

"Ed!" Heather squealed when she finally ID'd him. "What's up with you?"

"You tell me! You look like you just stepped out of the 'X-Files,'" he said.

"Oh, I guess I've got a few things on my mind," Heather responded, with a mysterious grin playing across her chapped lips.

"Yeah? Like what?" Ed wanted to know.

"Like Josh," she said, a little more stridently than she'd intended. "Things are going really great."

"Well, good." Ed bobbed his head, his urge to tease Heather flying out the window as he started to wonder if this was more than just a couple of rough nights for her. She was really acting skitzy. "I, uh—I hope he's treating you right. I noticed you hadn't been around much lately. . . ."

"Yeah, no worries," Heather said. She turned to him, leaned against the lockers, and peered at his face. "Wow, you look a little out of it. Is something going on?"

Ed decided not to note the irony of the new millennium: The walking bag of flotsam that was the former Heather Gannis was saying he looked out of it. All he knew was that he needed advice and that this little piece of the Heather he once knew peeking out at him was probably the best he could do for now.

"I am a little out of it," he admitted. "There's this thing that someone said to me, and I don't know if it could be true."

"If it's about Elvis being alive, I think you're out of luck," Heather told him. "The man is definitely gone for good."

"No, it's not that." Ed let out a whoosh of air, then leaned back against the lockers, too. He toyed with the metal extensions that seemed like part of his arm at this point. "It's kind of embarrassing," he admitted.

"More embarrassing than that time you laid a

giant fart during the assembly in third grade?" Heather asked.

"No. Not more embarrassing than that." Ed laughed. "All right. I went to physical therapy this morning, and instead of my regular guy, it was this chick."

"'Dear *Penthouse Forum,*'" Heather said. "'I never thought it would happen to me. . . .'"

"No, nothing like that," Ed said. He looked down. This was too hard for him to say. "She told me that— she told me I could walk without my crutches, and the only thing stopping me is that I'm afraid."

He looked up again and saw a strange look pass across Heather's face. *Oh, great.* She thought he was full of crap, or a big fake, or a coward. . . . He shouldn't have said anything.

"Ed." She put a hand on his arm and squeezed. "You *can't* be afraid."

"Yeah, I know, but I tried it this morning and I failed miserably. Fell flat on my face."

"Ed!" Now Heather had both hands on him, squeezing his upper arms and looking into his eyes with an intensity he had never seen in her. "If this physical therapist said you can walk, then it's true. The only reason you're not walking, the only reason you fell today, is because you're scared. Don't be such a wuss, Ed."

"Hey!" Ed shouted, though he wasn't sure whether

he was objecting to the fact that she had called him a wuss or the fact that she was crushing his bones.

"No!" Heather shook him. "Fear is bad. It's the worst thing in the world. It's the only thing stopping most people from living their lives. Don't you see that? Most of us can do anything we want—except our own doubt gets in our way. That's fear. Cut it out of you like a tumor, Ed. Fear is nothing but a trick. You're smarter than that."

"Uh, okay," he said in as calm a tone as he could muster. He didn't want to rile Heather up any more than he already had.

"Fear is bad. Being afraid sucks. And it's never going to happen to me again!"

Heather's voice was absolutely flat with determination. She gave Ed a final shove against the lockers and then walked away without another word. Ed didn't know what to think. Was the prom queen possessed? Was she drinking too much coffee? Most important, had she *meant* to use the word *wuss*?

In any case, she was starting to give Ed the heebie-jeebies, big time. She'd acted totally weird that day in the coffee shop, and now she was using Ed as a human drumstick. Whatever was going on in Ed's mind, something exponentially more freaky was going on in Heather's.

"Okay! Thanks a lot," he called, wondering whether there was anyone left still holding it together.

Hurricane of Onslaughts

CENTRAL PARK WAS THE ONLY GOOD thing about being uptown, as far as Gaia was concerned. Washington Square Park was really just a couple of city blocks. It had some nooks and crannies, but you could pretty much see it end to end from any angle. But this? A couple of miles of actual woodland in the middle of the city? It was pretty gorgeous.

Plus it provided her with infinitely more ass to kick.

The winding pathways and roads were even a little hard to navigate, despite her photographic-map-like memory. You could swear you were heading for Seventy-second Street and Strawberry Field, where the John Lennon garden was, and all of a sudden you ended up at Sixty-fourth, staring at Lincoln Center peeking out from a block away. Gaia loved the thrill of getting just slightly lost in the thick greenery, standing on a wide, flat rock surrounded by trees, even as the burps and backfires of massive delivery trucks on either side of the park were audible in the distance.

Not that this bucolic oasis, plopped smack in the middle of the city, was trouble-free. Was it only in New York that solitude of any kind meant the potential for danger was multiplied by ten? Gaia wondered. She stepped silently through a particularly dense piece of the park, and sure enough, before she could even take in the local flora, she heard the unmistakable sounds of a pack of guys hopped up on their own testosterone.

"Yo, man, where's all the sissies at today?" one of them yelled.

"Yoo-hoo, you want a piece of me?" another one called out.

Skinhead homophobes. Great! Gaia felt her senses sharpen as she tasted the potential for a good ass kicking. She hoped they were as stupid as they sounded.

She stepped farther into the trees and waited to see the group of goose steppers wander into her field of vision. Sure enough, they stepped out from between the trees, whacking at branches and laughing loudly. Just then a small man in pressed jeans, with carefully gelled hair and a Kenneth Cole backpack, wandered down the pathway. His footsteps slowed when he saw the pack of skinheads standing in his way.

"We thought we'd find someone like you here," the head guy said. He was a particularly gross example of the male species, with his sickly pale skin and orangy-red eyelashes. *If he'd invested in a tube of Clearasil instead of the oxblood Doc Martens he's wearing, his money would have been better spent,* Gaia thought.

"Look, I don't want any trouble." The guy took his backpack off his shoulder and retreated a few paces. "Do you want my wallet?"

"Your wallet? Man, I want your ass six feet under!"

That seemed to be the cue. The skinheads rushed the little guy, who turned around and ran with surprising speed. He wasn't fast enough, though, and one of the skinheads had grabbed him by the waistband and lifted him off the ground when Gaia leapt down on him from a tree branch above.

This was too good. Gaia shoved the little guy out of the way and yelled, "Run!" An order he was already obeying by the time it came out of her mouth. And then Gaia's body clicked into autopilot. If she saw a jaw, she smashed it. If she felt the breeze of a fist approaching her, she blocked it. The four men attacking her ceased to be individuals and became only body parts, a hurricane of onslaughts that Gaia dispatched with ease, one by one.

She could smell their aggression, their passion, their hatred and, as she felt the crunch of bone beneath her fist, their fear. That was where they lost. They were animals, humbled by their instinct, where Gaia, because she had no fear, was more like an efficient, logical machine.

Doosh. Someone came at her from behind, and she shoved an elbow upward, into his crotch.

Whap-smak. An ugly face said something rude, and she responded by whacking the heel of her hand up into his nose.

Kraaa-sploosh. Someone's blood spurted out of a fresh wound and across his buddy's T-shirt.

Ha. She wished all those yuppie gym-goers sweating it out in tae-bo-spinning-yoga-Pilates class could try this workout just once. It created quite a glow in a young lady.

Dum-dum-dum-dum-dum. . . Gaia suddenly felt an absence of aggression and heard retreating footsteps. She whirled around, hands out, making sure this wasn't just a lull in the battle.

"Aw, come on, guys. Gone so soon?" she called out. Three of the skinheads were racing away from her at top speed, and a fourth was stumbling, trying to run despite the fact that his broken nose was making his eyes gush with tears.

"Come back! I was just getting warmed up!"

But all her request did was light a fire under the last guy's ass, and he took off double time after his friends. Gaia was left alone in the park.

Of course, the battle over, her body began to rebel against her. She felt the familiar draining of all energy from her limbs. Gaia stumbled down the pathway, looking for a park bench, hoping to find someplace to plant herself where she wouldn't look like a vagrant while recovering from her fight.

In front of her she saw a big clearing and a large brown building. In front of it was a metal railing and a bunch of benches. As the edges of her consciousness began to fade, a rushing sound like a waterfall whooshed into her ears. She made a tunnel-vision beeline for the closest bench and collapsed onto it just as her limbs went cold and her knees turned to jelly.

She lay motionless for many minutes until her body gave her the signal it was time to wake up. It felt like every nerve ending, every blood vessel, every organ was gathering together to get her attention. She imagined them all meeting up near her spleen, complaining about how she was overusing them all during those intense physical confrontations and going on strike immediately afterward so they had a chance to regenerate.

Then her conscious mind finally kicked into gear, interrupting her weird dreamy reverie. *Hey. Hello. Pull it together, Gaia. You've been out for almost ten minutes.*

She opened her eyes and saw the same blank white sky, felt the hard wooden slats of the bench under her back. She wiggled her fingers and toes, then flexed her arms and legs, checking for any damage.

Bruises? Of course. Broken bones? Not a one—not

even a rib. She was going to be stiff for a while, though. She sat up and looked around her. She was farther uptown than she had thought and farther west, too: this was the Delacorte Theater, where people lined up during the summer to see free Shakespeare in an outdoor setting.

Just outside the front of the brown building was a bronze statue of a thin, wraithlike girl in a flowy dress dancing with some dude in a hat. Gaia squinted at it as she sat slumped on the bench, idly reading the inscription at the bottom. Romeo and Juliet. The star-crossed lovers whose love for each other caused them both to lose their lives.

Great, thought Gaia. *Very romantic.* Boy meets girl, boy's family has a fit about girl's family, and forces outside of their control conspire to keep them apart no matter how much they care about each other. And this was considered the greatest romance of all time? No wonder the world was such a screwy place.

As it always did, Gaia's mind wandered back to Ed. No question, he was the total love of her life. Also no question that being close to Gaia was going to doom him to total annihilation. Obvious answer? Stay the hell away from him, no matter how it flattened her own heart.

Damn. A broken bone would have been so much easier for Gaia to endure than a broken heart.

OLD HABITS ARE HARD TO BREAK.

Blissed— Out Grins

That was supposed to be an undeniable law of human nature, but Tom was finding that certain old habits were sloughing off him like skin from a molting snake.

Maybe the saying should have been, Old habits are hard to break, unless someone really wanted to get rid of them all along.

For example, his habit of always being alone. His habit of never trusting anyone. His habit of never, ever losing himself to pleasure, passion, and enjoyment of life. That was a habit he'd picked up after the death of his wife, to protect the safety of the daughter he cherished. And he hadn't realized how much he wanted to let it go until he'd met Natasha.

With an entire day at their disposal, at first they'd felt as giddy as children. Should they loll around in bed? Order up room service and feed each other bonbons? That, of course, was the last thing either of them really wanted to do. Part of their intense connection was their shared need to get out, to do, to accomplish things.

It turned out they were both scuba certified.

They found a local named Ted who had a boat and all the equipment on hand to motor them out to a bay where tourists didn't usually get to go. The ride was choppy, but the wind was cool on their faces, and they held each other, sitting on life jackets, as they watched the shoreline spool past.

It had been a while since Tom had gone deep. When they reached the bay, it was as picturesque as he had imagined. It actually kind of looked like the opening shot from *Gilligan's Island,* now that Tom thought about it, but he didn't want to make such a goofy reference.

"My God," Natasha said.

"What?" he asked.

"It's too stupid," she told him. "But I was thinking, this cove looks familiar, like this television show where the people are lost on the island and one woman is a movie star?"

Tom kissed her.

They both belted themselves into the devastatingly heavy air tanks, and Natasha hung several extra weights on her lithe frame to keep her from bobbing to the surface accidentally. They strapped their feet into the long flippers—horribly clumsy on the deck of the boat but absolutely essential and graceful under the water. And they spit into their masks.

"When I first was told to do this, I thought it was so disgusting." Natasha laughed, rubbing the gooey saliva across the inside of her blue mask. "But there's really no other way to keep it clear. Besides, it's my spit—I guess it can go in my face."

"Where did you learn to dive?" Tom asked. "I can't imagine Russia being an offshore destination."

"In Odessa it's pretty warm," she told him. "You have to wear a wet suit, but it's okay. Not like this, though." She looked around and sighed. "Are you boat sick?" she asked him.

"A little," he admitted. "It vanishes as soon as you jump in."

"Then let's go."

They both put their regulators in their mouths and fell backward into the water, floating at the surface at first, then regulating the pressure in their ears as they lowered themselves down the rope that hung off the edge of the boat.

Here, in the deep, there were no words, no need for explanations. The only communication was through hand signals. She gave him the okay sign once they'd gotten a good thirty feet down, and he reciprocated. Then they began paddling slowly, meditatively, around the beautiful, clear bottom of the ocean.

The sand was an eerie, glowing white down here, and if Tom reached down to touch it, his handprint puffed out like a footprint on the moon. The fish kept to themselves at first, but after a while they came over, a few at a time, then a great, overwhelming school of deep blue creatures.

Tom looked up. He could see the sky far, far away, like a dream he couldn't quite remember. And the whole time he heard his own breath, the steady, slow in and out of it filling his ears as it never did on the surface.

Natasha bonked him on the arm and pointed: Off in the distance a sea turtle was hovering, facing the other direction, waving its fins back and forth as if he were saying, "So-so, I'm doing so-so," over and over again. They tried to stealthily paddle closer to him, but the turtle was well attuned to changes in the underwater atmosphere. He flicked to the side just enough to eyeball them—and then took off like a lumbering bear, kerflapping away on his fins and disappearing into the murky depths. Natasha turned to Tom and shrugged. "Bashful," he could imagine her saying.

They paddled along silently, accompanied only by the sounds of their breathing. After a while Tom looked at his watch, double-checked his tank, and gave Natasha the thumbs-up signal. It was time to surface. They'd been down here as long as was safe, and they hadn't even realized it.

They slowly surfaced, carefully taking their time, and when their heads broke the top of the water, the real world seemed foreign and noisy, irritating and bright.

They plopped their flippers and masks on the deck and climbed up, squinting but with silly, blissed-out grins on their faces. Tom was pleased to note that

Natasha didn't say anything, not a word. It meant she felt the same way he did about coming out of a dive: like they had just left someplace sacred, and speaking too soon would ruin the moment.

They unclipped from their equipment, handed it all to Ted, and relaxed completely, lying on top of each other like a couple of flounders at a fish market, sighing with bliss at regular intervals. That is, until Natasha's cell phone shattered their peace with its shriek.

"Excuse me," she said, still smiling, and Tom noted that she turned away from him slightly as she answered.

"Hello? Yes. Yes. *Da.* Okay. I understand." She said a couple more words in Russian and then closed her phone. Tom looked at her expectantly, but she said nothing.

Something stirred inside Tom—something dormant, something he'd hoped would stay silent. *Old habits die hard,* he thought. He felt his old friend suspicion roll over, open its eyes, and tap the monitor next to its hospital bed. This particular habit wasn't quite dead yet: the habit of suspecting everyone, even those closest to you, of something nefarious.

He tried to smother it, but there it was: He was suspicious of Natasha. What was that phone call? Why didn't she fill him in? She just smiled, sat back, and acted like nothing had happened.

Well, maybe nothing had, Tom thought as he tried to return himself to his peaceful state.

Maybe.

Or maybe not.

EIGHTY BLOCKS DOWNTOWN, TATIANA sat in a stuffy classroom, trying to keep her mind on the calculus test she was supposed to be ready for. She scanned the page of formulas she had already memorized, making sure every x, y, and pi was burned into her brain, but her eyes wandered out the window. There was Heather, the perfect American girl, poised on the steps at the front of the school. The sun made a rainbow of highlights burst from her long, straight hair. And she always had a distinctive look. Lately she'd been going for that slept-in-her-clothes look, the one that usually only worked on Chloe Sevigny. But what really caught Tatiana's eye was the way Heather glowed from within, filled with joy and excitement.

Tatiana followed Heather's gaze and saw the most massively cute boy standing a few feet away, grinning back. God, he looked like he'd just stepped off a billboard: athletic build;

just-right jeans; a tailored, bowling-style shirt casually untucked; and a shock of silky black hair that brushed over his forehead. Heather walked slowly toward him and greeted him by first reaching a hand forward, then letting him draw her in slowly for a sensuous, full-lipped kiss.

A kiss like the one Ed had given her. After which, by the way, he seemed to have completely forgotten her phone number, e-mail address, and place of residence. Ed seemed to be totally avoiding her.

Oh God! Was Heather going to take off for a quickie at lunch? Tatiana burned with envy. She tore her eyes away from the decadent display in front of her and tried to focus on the numbers and letters on the page, but they were dancing around, deserting their regular places so they could run off together to the dark corners in the margin and make out. Sixes and nines hopped on top of each other in carnal abandon, and the ones and sevens were having a complete and total orgy with the y's. Ugh!

Tatiana let out a frustrated sigh. What she wouldn't give to be planted in one of the uncomfortable seats aboard Aeroflot, heading home to Russia right now. She'd spend the whole thirteen-hour flight scrunched between two fat Ukranians if it meant getting away from this stupid city with its annoying people.

Take Heather, for instance, who didn't even know

how amazing her life was: she was off somewhere making out with Josh Hartnett, and the only care she had in the world was whether to use gel or mousse when she blew out her hair. And Ed, who was so cute and charming and amazing, but would rather moon over the unattainable Gaia than admit that he and Tatiana would be a great couple. And of course Gaia, with all her possessions: boyfriend, beauty, and intelligence—Tatiana could tell she was incredibly sharp and smart, despite how she tried to hide it—Gaia was more interested in making everyone around her uncomfortable to the point of misery than in enjoying her life for even a moment.

It was enough to make Tatiana want to scream.

Everyone around her was blessed with everything they wanted, and here she was, stuck with a mom who was away half the time Lord knew where, a totally insane roommate, and a time-share boyfriend.

God bless America.

TATIANA COULDN'T TAKE IT ANY-more. She slammed her book shut, hearing the imaginary cries of the suddenly squished numbers and letters who'd

Handful of Ho Hos

just been having such a good time, and stood up.

The student lounge was empty except for a couple knotted together on one of the two seen-better-days couches along the wall, making out as if they'd just discovered these new things called lips and tongues. Tatiana hadn't even noticed them before.

Great. One more happy couple to add to my list.

She strode out of the lounge, out into the hallway, not even sure where she was headed. If Ed wanted to ignore her, then he could ignore her. But she wasn't going to make it easy for him. If he came face-to-face with the girl he'd kissed, wouldn't he have to say something? Wasn't there a law? And if not, was there a committee somewhere working to put it into the books?

Tatiana was determined to force some kind of confrontation. She knew she was being a little overly hyper, but then again, Ed had been a little overly friendly and was now a little overly avoiding her.

All right. So where was he? She knew he had AP history this period, but she wasn't sure what floor it was on. Anyway, she couldn't just go waltzing into his classroom and stand at the blackboard and announce that he was the kissing bandit. She had to be cool, run into him like it was an accident.

First floor. Wasn't AP history on the first floor? Taught by Mr. Verrinder. Yes! She raced down the stairs two at a time, hoping she wouldn't run into a hall monitor in her effort to make it down before the end of the period. Unless Ed was sent to the office at the same time, that would completely derail her plan.

The bell shrieked just as she arrived at the corner she had decided on, near the vending machines, and as the doors to all the classrooms slammed open in unison and began leaking high school kids, she straightened her sweater, tried to smooth her hair, and attempted to be convincing in her sudden interest in the choice between Bit-O-Honey and jujubes.

She spotted him out of the corner of her eye immediately. He was hard to miss, of course. His hitching gait as his crutches helped him along set him apart from the rest of the crowd. So did his adorably rumpled hair and his unconsciously cute way of wearing his shirt untucked. But he didn't seem to see her.

Tatiana gave the vending machine a thump with her fist, then kicked it. This was a silly scene to be making, but what was the English expression? Desperate times call for desperate measurements, or something like that.

"Give me my Ho Hos, you stupid machine," she said in a voice loud enough to make a few heads turn.

There. He looked up. And he was too close to get away with ignoring her.

She turned to face him as if she were just looking around for help. "Oh, Ed!" she cried out, with all the mock surprise of Bart Simpson finding out he was in trouble with Principal Skinner again. "I didn't expect to see you down here. Can you help me figure out this stupid machine?"

Ed's face betrayed no emotion—not surprise, not guilt, and not joy at seeing her.

Tatiana felt embarrassed and somehow naked, but it was too late to run away now.

Ed came over to the vending machine and studied it for a moment. "It says you didn't put money in," he pointed out. "It says zero cents up there."

Ugh. Sure enough, the bright red LED display said zero point zero zero.

"Oh, but I did put the money in," she complained. "That is why this machine is so stupid. I put the money in, but it didn't register somehow."

Without a word, Ed reached into the pocket of his jeans, pulled out sixty cents, and dropped the coins in. The numbers leapt, and Tatiana's face burned.

"It looks okay now," he said. "Were you trying to unload your rubles again?"

Tatiana gave a shrill laugh, a ridiculous sound that bubbled out of her without her consent. "Ha ha! Yes, perhaps I was using rubles," she said, hitting the Ho Hos button for want of anything better to do. She turned to Ed.

"So, how are you?" she asked. "I have not spoken to you in a while."

"I'm okay." *Aha.* Was that what she thought it was? A look of embarrassment? Was he looking at the floor because he knew he'd screwed up? He had to apologize now. She had him! He totally had to. . .

"Well, see you later," he said, replacing his crutches under his arms and hitching away from her without another word.

Oh my God, Tatiana thought. *He hates me. I must be the worst kisser in the world!*

No. He is the biggest jerk in the world!

Either way, she was the definitely most embarrassed person in the world, standing in a high school hallway with a handful of Ho Hos and a heart full of hurt.

This place sucked.

Yes. All right. I admit it. That was bad. Horrible, in fact. Maybe the primo worst move of my life. I'd kick myself if I could figure out how. Obviously I'm avoiding Tatiana, and I'm doing it with all the smoothness of George Constanza. But I have a lot on my mind.

First, my physical therapist informs me that, like Dorothy in *The Wizard of Oz*, I've had the power to get what I've wanted all along—I just didn't know how to use it. Heartwarming words. Then I try out her theory and literally fall flat on my face. So I pour my heart out to my old friend Heather, who, admittedly, was a poor choice of confidante since she's obviously got some completely weird emotional trauma of her own going on that makes her look like half a Heather. And so she goes all Mariah Carey on me.

Then I stop by the main office right before history class and find out Gaia's not in school

today. Not that I care. Not that
Gaia matters to me at all. But
that girl has a way of attracting
danger. I'm just a little
concerned.

And this whole time I'm supposed to be concentrating on Ed.
Do you see why I don't exactly
have the time or energy to be
calling some chick I smooched?

Oh God. Did I just say that? I
didn't mean it. Tatiana is an
absolutely great girl, not some
chick, and I smooched her because
I meant it. And the not-so-unspo-
ken rule of being a half-decent
guy is, even if you didn't mean
it, you call a girl after you
stick your tongue down her
throat. I mean, if she was willing to risk mono for you, you
pretty much owe her that, right?
If you're not interested, you let
her know by saying you'll call
again. She'll usually get the
picture.

But you've got to make the
first call.

And what kind of idiot

wouldn't be interested in
Tatiana? She's absolutely perfect. Her body is smokin'—and her
features are delicate, like a
china doll's. And sweet. And
friendly. No obnoxious comments
bursting out of her mouth. No
need to be on your guard with
her. Tatiana. Of course I'm
interested.

It's just with all the bizarro
events of the last week, I need a
little "Ed time" right now.

I am going to call her eventually. I'll owe her big time—I
might have to treat her to something schmantzy, like a concert
or something, to make it up to
her. I'll just explain to her
that I needed to figure some
things out.

If I ever figure things out.

When things come together this perfectly, it's very difficult not to congratulate myself. My own genius astounds even me.

I've managed to twist the brilliant Gaia into a knot of confusion. I have her believing every word I say. She is convinced that Natasha is a double agent, and she can't even figure out who her own father is. All because of my manipulation. Soon she'll be my pawn: it's so delicious, having her in my grasp.

And Heather. The beautiful fool. How easy it is to twist the mind of a young, impressionable girl simply by tugging on her heartstrings. What possible purpose could this total malleability have? Why did it develop in adolescent humans? Do they have no minds of their own? Whether it's devotion to the Backstreet Boys or a passion for a black stallion, the average sixteen-year-old girl would rather latch onto a faraway ideal than develop a single idea for herself.

LOKI

This one especially. She considers herself an iconoclast, but look how I've drawn her into my web of deceit.

She is going to be a magnificent subject for my experiment. I'll be able to test the fearless serum on her: she is ready and willing to try it. In fact, if it works, she might turn out to be an even better operative than Gaia. Gaia, after all, did not have the opportunity to choose her fearless state: it was nothing more than an accident, a mysterious mutation that occurred in her mother's womb. And Gaia seems to spend her life cursing her fate, fighting against her status instead of embracing it and allowing herself to become the magnificent creature she has the potential to be.

Heather, on the other hand, knows exactly what she's getting into. She's lived a life cursed by the shadow of fear, so when she sloughs it off, she'll taste all the more piquantly the joy of

fearlessness. Even now, it seems
as if she is without a conscience. Could it be that her
view of life—unencumbered by a
concern for others, however
feigned that attitude may be—
could be even more useful? Match
that with an absence of cowardli-
ness, and she'll be positively
unstoppable.

A magnificent machine: the
ultimate weapon, acting completely at my will.

It won't be long now.

You know what? I've realized something. We're all given a choice in this life. We can take the well-worn path laid out before us and proceed to live a preapproved life that contains no surprises, no curveballs, and no challenges.

Or we can step off the path and make our own way.

Take Francis Ford Coppola. I just saw an A&E special on him. Everyone thought he was a lunatic when he made *Apocalypse Now*. He vanished into the jungle, mortgaged his own house to pay for this bloated, overbudget mess of a movie, and uprooted his whole family for a year or better. And everyone swore it would be a flop. Surprise: It swept the Oscars and changed the face of modern cinema.

History is littered with the corpses of those who rejected everyone's expectations, stepped out of line, and made a break for something greater. I'm not an

H E A T H E R

idiot. I know I'm taking a hell
of a chance.

But you know what? I'm tired
of being afraid. I'm tired of
timidly hiding behind a mask of
MAC, making up a face to look
like everyone else. Look at Ed.
He's so scared, he doesn't even
know he can walk. That will never
be me. And my family, for God's
sake—my sister, who's so insecure
she's literally starving herself,
and my parents, who've bled themselves dry trying to keep up with
the Joneses. I can't let that
happen to me. I want to stand
out. I want to leave mediocrity
behind. And if I burn bright
enough to catch a few eyes before
I wink out of sight entirely,
then so be it: at least I made an
impression.

I'm going to do this thing.
I'm going through with the experiment. Let them shoot me up with
whatever they want: I'm ready to
take the chance.

The wiseass attitude had gone from being a **mental** hobby to necessity. **stench** And he liked it that way.

"THANKS FOR PICKING ME UP,"

Heather said, relaxing into Josh's embrace in front of the school. She barely gave a glance behind her as she took his hand and strolled up the street with him. She could get expelled for cutting class like this, but this was the new Heather: daring, nonchalant, and—almost—fearless. "I wasn't sure that you got my message."

Irony

"Of course I did," Josh told her, waving his cell phone. "It was crazy; I didn't hear it ring, but something told me to look at it and there you were, in my voice mail in-box."

Heather laughed. "Yeah, I have a way of getting attention," she said.

Josh squeezed her hand. "Mine, anyway." She smiled at him, and he felt something flip over in his chest. "So what was so important that you decided to waste your parents' precious tuition dollars?"

"I wanted to tell you something," Heather said. They reached Washington Square Park, and she sat him down on a bench, facing her, with her hands on his shoulders. She stepped into the space between his feet and looked deeply into his piercing blue eyes.

"I'm ready," she told him. "I want to do this. And I want to do it as soon as possible."

Josh laughed. "It sounds like you're propositioning me," he said. "Anyone listening to this conversation would be quite shocked by you, Heather Gannis."

"Please, this is so much bigger than sex." Heather shook her head, smiling like someone who'd just had a religious conversion. "What you're offering me is precious, and I'm lucky I met you, so you could hook me up with this amazing experiment. I thought over everything you said to me, and I don't know why I didn't see it before. It makes total sense. If it wasn't a risk, it wouldn't have such an amazing payout. If I stand around asking questions, then I'm no better than the ordinary people who never take a chance. But I *am* better than them, and I want to make this leap of faith. Josh, I want to be fearless."

Josh broke their gaze first as a shadow crossed his face. He took her hand and kissed her fingers, frowning.

"What's wrong?" Heather asked him. "I thought you'd be happy. I thought this was what you wanted."

"I just want to be sure it's what *you* want," Josh said, still unable to meet her gaze. "I'm not sure you've thought it all through. There are risks involved—terrible risks."

"Hello! Josh, are you in there?" She knocked on his skull. "Haven't you heard what I've been saying? Nothing worth doing is completely safe."

"I'm just worried that you—"

"Worried!" Heather laughed and hugged him, pulling

his head into her chest. "You are so sweet. Josh, I'm a big girl. I'm totally excited to do this. I'm going to be just what you said, a bright and shining creature. And you're the one who gave me this chance."

She leaned in for a long, reassuring kiss. "I know what's really going on," she whispered.

"And what's that?" he asked.

"You're afraid you'll lose me when I'm this all-new girl. But you won't. I'll never forget that if it wasn't for you, I would never have been part of this experiment."

She swept her arms around him and gave him a huge, grateful hug. Josh patted her back, feeling how thin she had become, how fragile her little bones seemed.

"You're sure you want to do this?" he said.

"I insist on doing it," she told him.

Her words echoed in his mind. *If it wasn't for you, I would never have been part of this experiment.*

He drew back, took Heather by the shoulders, and looked at her. "I don't want you to do this," he said flatly. "I can't tell you why, exactly. But I've figured out a way to get you out of town. You can stay with friends of mine in Woodstock. Lay low for a while, and I'll find someone else to be Oliver's guinea pig. You don't need to do this. You don't need anything, Heather. You're perfect just the way you are."

Heather turned to him with a concerned and wary look on her face. "Josh, you're acting really weird," she told him. "What's going on? Why are you saying all this?"

"Because I know more about it than you do," he said, stopping short of telling her exactly how deadly the experiment could be. He had to be cautious. One false step now and she could mistrust him completely—write him off as a nutcase. He just hoped he was touching that part of her that was still unsure about proceeding with the experiment.

"Stop it, you're freaking me out," she said angrily.

Uh-oh. Whatever he was touching, it seemed to be a raw nerve, not a kernel of reason.

"Listen to me, Heather." Josh gripped her shoulders with both hands, looking intensely into her eyes. He could not let her endanger herself. His heart was thumping, and he felt desperate with the need to force her to see reason. She was running across the train tracks with a massive Amtrak engine bearing down on her: He had to save this girl from her own desire for self-destruction.

"Ouch!" she said, drawing backward.

"Listen to me," he repeated. "This isn't safe. You have to leave town. I've even found you a ride. You don't need clothes; we can find anything you need on the ride up there. Hell, you go right past the outlet stores. I don't want you taking this injection. I won't allow it. I forbid it."

Whoops. Too late, Josh realized he'd said just the thing that would turn Heather Gannis off completely.

"You won't what?" she intoned, sounding like an angry queen. Josh let go of her arms, giving her sleeves a friendly little straightening out as he sat back slightly and retracted his intense rays as best he could.

"I didn't mean that," he said meekly.

"You're damn right you didn't mean that," she told him. "Nobody—not even my parents—'forbids' me to do anything."

Quick, Josh—think. You're losing all credibility.

"Of course they don't. You think I don't know who I'm dealing with here? I was just testing you," he said with a rush of laughter, knowing he had to get her to forgive him. Knowing he had to stay close to her. If he couldn't keep her away from this experiment, he had to keep watch over her, protect her as well as he could.

She gave him a curious look. Was she buying it? She had to; Josh's ability to keep her safe hinged on how he played this one.

"Come on, Heather!" He laughed again. "You can't be this gullible! I was just making sure that you really wanted to do this. That you weren't going to freak out at the last minute."

There was a tension-filled moment as he saw her turning this over in her mind. He gave his most reassuring smile. Then, to his relief, she gave one back.

"Ohmigod, you really fooled me," she said, smacking him on the shoulder.

"I'm sorry, pretty girl," he said, drawing her into a warm hug and kissing her on the forehead. "Come on, I owe you something for putting you through that little performance. Let's go to Borgia's, and I'll treat you to a tiramisu."

The thought of a creamy Italian dessert more than made up for a few minutes of inappropriate intensity, apparently. Heather stood and took his hand, as trusting as she'd ever been. Josh led her across to the west side of the park. The irony of it was twisting his intestines into knots.

She trusted him, as long as he was leading her into danger. The minute he tried to keep her safe, she was ready to run away from him.

He was just going to have to let this play out and save her in some other way. He hoped he could. He had a bad feeling her life depended on it.

A Faint, Satisfying Click

THERE WAS NOTHING LIKE THE FEELing of being on assignment and having everything click into place, Tom thought. He had spent his life working on endless cases, and each one had its own personality. Some were sluggish and unwilling to break, and working them was like slogging through mud. Some were amusing, with clues popping out of the strangest places. But rarely, if ever, had he felt so in control and satisfied with how things were going. It reminded him of why he had chosen this line of work in the first place.

Dressed to the nines in a slick Armani suit, with Natasha on his arm in a dress that defied the laws of physics, Tom Moore was the very picture of a high-rolling playboy out to lose a couple thousand at the roulette table. The Caribbean was known for its lax gambling rules, but when so much money was at stake, all eyes were on the chips on the table, including those of the eye-in-the-sky camera poised above them. There was no room for error; fortunately, he and Natasha made a perfect team, and no errors were made.

From the regular casino they could hear the clanging of slot machines and the distant rumble of thousands of people murmuring, an occasional cheer or roar of defeat punctuating the white noise. But here in the lush back room, the walls were a deep burgundy velvet, and the mood was much more subdued. The wheel spun with a smooth series of clicks as the ball made its way around the red and black numbers to rest on one.

Tom and Natasha were not here for recreation, though they laughed and gambled like a couple of old-school players from a Frank Sinatra movie. They barely sipped the cocktails served to them and carefully watched their mark, three seats down from them at the roulette table.

His name was Fenster, and Tom could tell he was a total and complete nerd. Glasses, balding, sickly skin—he was the real deal. Guys like that should at least do something for a living that was unexpected, but no: he was an accountant. Loki's accountant. A high-level number cruncher who was here in the Cayman Islands to watch Loki's bank accounts and move his money around at different intervals, to keep it one step ahead of the international authorities.

But even a high-level number cruncher had to blow off steam sometimes, right?

Tom's operative had given him the tip-off earlier in the day, and he and Natasha had sprung into action. Their intention was just to watch this guy and wait for him to slip up. Enough patience, and he certainly would. And sure enough, the more he drank, the more money he bet. *Getting sloppy,* Tom thought. *It won't be long now.*

"You know what, I'm going to put it all on the double zero," he said to Natasha.

"This is so boring. Can't we play craps?" Natasha moaned, the very picture of sultry lethargy.

"Come on, baby! You know I like the numbers," Tom told her, relishing the role that let him step out of his usual taciturn nature. He slid a pile of bright red chips onto the green number all the way at the tip of the table and watched the wheel spin. It came up nineteen-red.

"Damn!" he said with a laugh. "I could have bought a small island with that."

"No matter," Natasha purred, bending over and nuzzling his ear. "There's plenty more where that came from, right, baby?"

"You bet," Tom told her, toying with his chips in expert fashion. With one hand he lifted the stack. . . split it in two. . . shuffled the chips. . . returned them to one stack. It was a smooth-looking party trick, a subtle use of his hands, but it caught people's attention nonetheless. Helped him into his role. The warmth he felt emanating from Natasha's body helped him relax into character.

"You're all over the place," Fenster chided him from his end of the table. "You don't know what you want to play. That's no way to win. You've got to be consistent."

"Consistency was never my strong suit," Tom responded, looking down the table at Fenster, who was greedily taking in the luscious Natasha even as he spoke to Tom. "But you sound like a man who knows what he's talking about."

"Oh, I am," Fenster squeaked, bouncing up and down in his chair ever so slightly. "I play my good-luck numbers. Stick to 'em, and they always pay out. It's a question of averages."

Hmmm. Plays his favorite numbers, does he? That was when Tom noticed that Fenster's green chips were ranged over the same pattern of numbers on every spin. All he had to do was glance at Natasha to know she'd seen it, too. He saw her concentrated stare as she memorized the series of numbers in her steel-trap, photographic memory.

"Slow and steady, is that your game?" Tom asked. "You never take a chance on something unexpected?"

The chair next to his was vacated as a small fortune was lost on one roll and the man who'd lost it threw his hands in the air and retreated to the craps table. Natasha oozed into the chair, sensuously descending, aware that all eyes—not just Fenster's and Tom's—were upon her.

"That's right," Fenster told him. "All that crazy betting is going to cost you in the long run. It's bad business!"

"And your business, it is a good business?" Natasha asked, her accent—or the accent of the woman she was pretending to be—as thick as the fog on a mountaintop in the Urals.

"My business is an excellent business," Fenster said with conviction. "In fact. . ." He let loose a high-pitched giggle. Tom noticed a slight tightening in Natasha's jawline at the unexpected noise and almost had to laugh out loud. "I'd probably take better care of someone like you than that crazy-betting guy you're with. At least I'm dependable!"

"You better watch it, my friend," Tom intoned, concentrating on the liquid movement of the chips in his hand as he bet a stack on number eleven. "This lady's very special to me."

"Oh, don't be such a muddy stick," Natasha chided him. "He is just being friendly."

97

"All right, doll," Tom murmured, with just a hint of threat in his voice. "Go be friendly, then."

"Perhaps I will," Natasha pouted, her bottom lip growing a full half inch as she slipped out of her chair and seemingly floated down to Fenster.

Tom watched her, outwardly playing the somewhat jealous sugar daddy, inwardly feeling a fiery rush of admiration for the skillful way she was manipulating the poor fellow.

"Tell me about your steady game," she told Fenster, sliding Tom a reproachful glance.

Nice touch, he thought. He watched her run an ivory hand up Fenster's hairy, beet red arm and felt a shiver of—what? Jealousy? No, he wasn't worried that Natasha would go too far in her assignment. He simply wanted her for himself. At the same time, he wished everyone in the room could know what she was up to—so they could admire her as he did.

Fenster didn't stand a chance.

Natasha murmured something into Fenster's ear and made him titter again, ordering him a big, fruity drink served in a ceramic tiki god festooned with umbrellas. He said something back to her, something that made her look sharply at Tom, dropping character for less than a nanosecond. She had something. Something they could use. He received the information with a jolt, and then she was gone again, vanished back into the vapid creature she was pretending to be.

God, he adored her.

This was what he'd always wanted. Work and personal life coming together as elegant as a tango. Working with a partner might be a good idea after all.

"The secret is in the chips," Fenster was telling Natasha. "It's not the numbers themselves. It's about the relationship between them. You follow?"

"I follow you anywhere, cutie pie!" Natasha purred.

"You don't understand a word I'm saying, do you?" Fenster laughed.

"I understand," she said, giggling.

"I'm warning you, my friend," Tom said. "She's smarter than you think."

"I'll bet she is," Fenster crowed, daring to give her hip a nasty pinch. Natasha gave a squeal and pretended to slap his hand away as she laughed, but Tom could see she was dreaming of snapping his idiotic head clean off. "She's smart, all right. Smart enough to fetch me another drink, right, baby?"

"I get you a drink later," she told him, grinning as she realized that he suspected nothing. "I better go back to my big man over there before he comes and gets me himself."

"Aw, don't go—" Now it was Fenster's turn to pout. His eyes devoured Natasha as she strutted away from him, and he gave her what he surely thought was a secret, just-between-us wink. Which she returned, politely.

"I think we make a good team," Tom whispered to Natasha, allowing himself a moment of truth between their elaborate lies.

"Maybe you're right," she responded. "But you know, we'll have to let some others in on our secret if we want to take this all the way."

Once again, she'd practically read his mind. There was no doubt that they were passionately, emotionally in sync. And no doubt that the heat between them made a forest fire look like a Yule log. Tom wanted Natasha to help him glue together the fractured fragments of his life. Once she helped him get rid of Loki, she could surely help him rediscover how to be a father to Gaia. As soon as they finished this assignment, they'd have to hightail it back to New York City and admit to their daughters that they were in love.

OKAY. SO. YEAH. *THE CRUTCHES HAVE got to go.*

Ed stood on the roof of his building, breathing in the air and trying to convince himself that he really didn't need the

Voices from the Sky

metal contraptions backing up his pathetically weak leg muscles.

The thing was, no matter what his brain said, his legs were pretty sure it was full of hooey.

Just last week he had clattered down four flights of stairs with his crutches. He'd needed desperately to get down quickly, with a minimum of fuss. If ever he was going to have some big, TV-movie-style breakthrough, that really would have been a good time. But his thigh muscles had been just as dull and stubborn as always. So why would this be any different?

Well, his brain said, *because now you know Lydia said your legs are fine, so you can just move on from the whole helpless thing.*

Okay. But Lydia might be full of crap. She might be an escaped mental patient posing as a physical therapist to get her jollies. In which case Ed was going to toss out two hundred dollars' worth of medical equipment and spend the evening scrootching down a flight of stairs on his skinny skate-kid ass for no good reason at all.

He sighed. It was do-or-die time. If he wasn't going to toss the crutches, he might as well shove them back onto his arms, return downstairs, and catch another "Real World in San Francisco" rerun.

But that was too much to bear. No way could he bear to watch Puck go off on that poor guy Pedro again.

Ed closed his eyes, took a breath, and gave a little "oof" as he hoisted his crutches over the side of the roof. There were a few seconds of silence, and then he heard them crash into the crud-filled Dumpster below.

There was no getting them back now. He turned around, stepped forward confidently, felt his left knee buckle, and landed smack with his face against the aluminum-colored tar of the roof.

He lay there for a moment, tasting rubber, working his jaw. This was going to be interesting.

He rolled onto his back and looked up at the setting sun.

"Am I out of luck? Or can I really do this? he asked the heavens.

There was no answer, which was kind of a relief since the last thing Ed needed was to start hearing voices from the sky. Bad enough he had a face full of grime and a seriously wounded ego.

And a mental block that was screwing up his life beyond belief.

The more he thought about it, the more it seemed right to him, what his physical therapist had said. His whole life had changed when he had his accident. Before, he'd been Shred, the footloose skater who refused to take anything seriously. That was what had gotten him into trouble, really—his inability to stand up to Heather and her bitchy friends, to be serious enough to say, "What, are you kidding? If I skate that hill, I'll end up in a wheelchair."

So instead of opening his mouth, he'd skated the hill. And ended up in a wheelchair.

Which had changed him completely. Sure, he was still Ed, still the wiseass. But he saw how the world had changed in response to him. Heather had peeled off and broken up with him. His sister, embarrassed by his paraplegic status, had faded from his life. The pain of that had given him a reason to step back—well, wheel back—and had helped him put up defensive walls between himself and everyone close to him. The wiseass attitude had gone from being a hobby to a necessity. And he'd liked it that way. He'd felt safer.

Maybe he'd been using the chair, and later the crutches, to keep himself from going back to the old Ed, the stupid and trusting Ed who thought that just because you loved people, that meant they'd stick by you.

Maybe what he really wanted was for Gaia to show up and cheer him on.

Maybe he had to accept the fact that he was going to have to rescue himself. And promise himself that if he could get his legs to work, he'd keep rescuing himself and move on from wiseass Ed and scared Ed to some kind of third Ed. A new and better Ed.

"All right? A new and better Ed," he promised out loud.

He hoped someone heard him. Because if not, he was going to have a hell of a time getting downstairs.

TATIANA'S MOOD WAS ABSOLUTELY

rancid as she cleaned her room for the umpteenth time. No matter what she did, she couldn't seem to get the mental stench of Gaia out of her room. There was no dirt, there was no actual odor; it was the aura, she supposed, of that grouchy, weird girl that seemed to pervade

Mother–Defending Fury

the air even after she took Gaia's stuff out to the living room.

Oh, who was she kidding. Tatiana knew exactly what was wrong with her, and it had nothing to do with Gaia. Ed still hadn't called. He'd kissed her, held her, *used* her, and hadn't even bothered to pick up the phone to ask her out again. Or give her the old heave-ho like a man. No, she was expected to figure out, from the silence, that he just wasn't interested.

Real great, Ed, she thought. *Very gentlemanly.*

It didn't help that bitch-*meister* Gaia was the real

object of his affections. Tatiana would never be able to figure that one out. Gaia was awful. She had dumped Ed. She had no interest in him. Yet Ed preferred this awful girl to Tatiana, who truly cared for him.

And there was no hope of getting rid of her—not as long as their parents remained locked in whatever idiotic romance they were in. Of all people her mother could date, why Gaia's father?

The whole situation was starting to stress her out beyond belief.

"Speaking of the devil," she said out loud to herself as she heard the front door of the apartment open and slam shut. Even Gaia's footsteps sounded hostile. Tatiana stepped to the door of her room and glared at her.

"So now you are a hooker?" she asked.

Gaia stopped in her tracks. "What?" she snapped.

"From school. You played hooker today. You were not in your classes."

Gaia's face broke into a smile for approximately three seconds.

"Hooky! I played hooky. Jeez, Tatiana, you should at least know what your insults mean before you toss them at me."

"Oh." Tatiana felt stupid. And the smile, which had opened Gaia's face so beautifully, was gone as quickly as it had appeared, as if she had yanked down a garage door over her true feelings. "Well, I think you are supposed to attend school."

"I thought we were splitting up the apartment so we wouldn't run into each other," Gaia said, avoiding the issue at hand. "Like, you stay out of my business and I stay out of yours?"

"I just think it is very irresponsible of you to skip classes," Tatiana said.

"Irresponsible?" This seemed to strike a chord with Gaia. "You have no idea what responsibilities I'm dealing with."

"Oh, what, the responsibility to make everyone around you feel miserable all the time?" Tatiana said, her hand on her hip as the sarcasm torpedoed out of her. "The responsibility to be the most unpleasant person on the planet? Or perhaps you feel responsible to give me an ulcer before my mother returns from her business trip?"

"Do me a favor and don't bring your mother into this," Gaia said. "I don't even want to think about that double-crossing bitch."

"All right. All right!" Tatiana stormed over to Gaia and stood in front of her. Gaia towered over her by a good several inches, glaring down like an icy Valkyrie. But Tatiana was too pissed to care. She suddenly had all the attitude of Li'l Kim being told her Armani towels would not be waiting backstage. In other words, she was absolutely radiating fury.

"You listen to me, Gaia Moore," Tatiana said, her voice quiet yet piercing in its fury. "You can insult me all you want. But when you insult my mother, you are stepping over the line. I will not stand for it. And yes, I am aware that you can kick my butt. You are bigger than me and you are a bully, so why don't you go ahead? I'd rather have a bloody nose than stand by and listen to you insult my mother again."

"Do yourself a favor and get the hell out of my face," Gaia told her, her face as impassive as a granite slab. "I could give you a lot worse than a bloody nose."

"And this is something you are proud of," Tatiana sneered. "It is revolting. I wish with all my heart that you and your slimy father would leave my mother and me alone."

"Look who's talking about slime," Gaia shot back. "My father might have horrible taste, but at least he's not a double-crossing snake."

"What are you talking about?" Tatiana demanded.

"What are *you* talking about?" Gaia echoed. "You think our parents are just having an innocent romance? Please. Why don't you grow up and see what's really going on?"

"Oh, and what is really going on, Gaia?"

"My father is a government agent, Tatiana," Gaia shouted, letting her secret spill from her lips, whooshing out, fueled by the fury that had taken over all her judgment. "An American government agent. And your mother is nothing but a filthy spy, sent here to seduce him—and then destroy him. Face it. She's a double-crossing sleazebag."

For a long moment Tatiana gazed into Gaia's eyes. Then, in an impressive display of adrenaline-fueled, mother-defending fury, Tatiana let loose a sucker punch of such immense proportions, it dropped Gaia to the floor like a featherweight in the ring with Mike Tyson.

Gaia blinked once. Her eyes rolled back in her head, her vision grew dark, and she thudded to the floor. She outweighed Tatiana. She was trained in the art of combat.

But she hadn't counted on Russian family loyalty.

She walked out of the school, toward home, **shrill** enjoying the **hum** speeded-up smoothness of her **in** thoughts and the intensely **her** saturated **head** colors of the world around her.

HEATHER DIDN'T EVEN HAVE TO look at the clock to know it was exactly three-thirty. She didn't need the clanging of the bell signaling the end of the school day, either. The shrill hum in her head was all she needed to know it was time for her next dose of pills.

Now that she'd gotten on a better schedule with them, though, she didn't look like crap all the time. She tossed four pills toward the back of her throat and downed them with a bottle of Evian. She knew that when Josh had first given her these pills, it had taken some time for her body to get used to them, and she hadn't known enough to take the next dose at the first sign of withdrawal. Now she had it down to a science.

She waited a moment, and the buzzing in her head ceased just as a warm tingle entered her veins, starting in her belly and radiating outward. *Boy, this stuff works fast,* she thought. When she took an Advil for her cramps, she could be writhing in pain for twenty minutes or more, but somehow these Josh pills entered her bloodstream almost instantly.

Whatever this stuff is, I could make a mint with it at Twilo.

But that wasn't why she was taking these pills. She hitched her backpack higher on her shoulder and walked out of the school, toward home, enjoying the speeded-up smoothness of her thoughts and the intensely saturated colors of the world around her. This wasn't just a pleasure trip, though she did enjoy the way the pills made her feel. But she wasn't just another spoiled rich kid getting back at Mummy and Daddy by developing a heroin habit or snorting coke in the maid's bathroom. These pills served a purpose—a serious one. They were prepping her for the ultimate transformation.

Josh had assured her that if she kept up her end of the bargain and filled her system with whatever was in the orange prescription bottle, her body would be all the more ready to receive the fearless infusion.

That was going to be fantastic. A life without fear? That would finally set her apart from all the annoying regular people around her. After all the time she'd put in playing the popular game, after all the hurt she'd felt in losing both Sam and Ed to Gaia and all the suffering she'd gone through with her family, it was totally what she deserved.

Enough of this everyday-living shit for her. Heather wanted to be plucked from obscurity and given something that would set her apart forever.

And unlike Gaia, she'd know how to use her power.

Heather was so caught up in her thoughts, she didn't watch where she was going. She stepped onto Eighth Street right in front of a yellow taxicab, which blared its horn at like eight million decibels and scared her half to death. She jumped right out of her skin.

"Hey!" she shouted, her heart thudding in her chest. "Watch it!"

The cabdriver only laughed his stinky head off. He put the car in neutral and gunned the engine, which made Heather do the panicked spaz jump-run out of his way. The cabdriver laughed even harder.

Perv. He probably got his thrills from scaring girls on every corner. Heather hated herself for having shown how startled she was. In response, she stood on the corner and held out a beautifully manicured middle finger at the cabdriver as he drove off.

Okay, jackass, she thought. *You got me once. But you'll never scare me again.*

THE CAYMAN ISLANDS HAD PROBABLY

never seen such a beautiful day. Even in a part of the world known for its endless succession of stunning, warm, lush

The Altar of Macintosh

tropical beauty, this was a doozy. The sun glinted on the water, the air was the perfect balmy temperature, and the clouds looked like they had been hand-designed by Martha Stewart.

None of which mattered to Tom and Natasha. They were holed up in their hotel room with the curtains drawn, dressed in sweats and T-shirts, downing cup after cup of black coffee.

Notepads scribbled with numbers were strewn across the bed, and their two laptops were working overtime, straining their logic boards to keep up with the frantic pace of the two government operatives. This was more than just a question of national security. Tom was fighting for his daughter's life—and his relationship to her in it—and he was not about to be distracted by anything.

"We have all of these numbers," Natasha grumbled, looking at the scrawled digits. "But how do they go together? What do they mean?"

"They've got to be the key to Loki's numbered bank accounts," Tom responded. "Come on, keep feeding them into the system. We have to hit the right combination one of these times."

Natasha gave a frustrated sigh and sat up tall, arching her back to loosen the aching kinks that were plaguing her. "This is too time-consuming," she said. "Give me a moment. I have an idea."

Tom heard the pattern of her typing change—suddenly it was fluid, energetic, unlike the frustrated tapping of the number keys that had defined the previous few hours.

"What are you doing?" he asked.

"I am writing a quick program," she said. "I can hack into the bank's internal server and design an input module that will try the numbers for us in different combinations, as if we were entering them ourselves."

Tom watched Natasha's fingers fly over the keys as she entered a dizzying amount of code. She cursed a few times, glaring at the screen as her program tanked a few times and restarting the computer once when it crashed in response to her warp-speed typing. After about ten minutes, though, she gave a sharp cheer and clapped. He looked over her shoulder at a neat box in the corner of the screen. She entered the numbers from the notepads and hit a button. The box began spinning like a slot machine, trying every combination of the numbers, beeping as it rejected each new selection.

"Now we just sit back and let it work," she said. "Much easier, no?"

"Much easier, yes," Tom said. "I can't believe you just did that. You're better than the guys back at headquarters."

"Indeed, I am much better than the guys at headquarters," Natasha agreed. She stretched like a kitten and relaxed, watching the screen intently. It gave an angry buzz, and she cursed again.

"You're going to have to teach me some of those," Tom told her.

"I think you are going to learn them before too long," Natasha replied. "Damn, damn, damn. I thought the numbers he was playing were the numbers of the bank account. I thought for sure this was the case. But I've tried them in every combination, and they don't work."

17. 24. 13. 36. 0. 34. The numbers danced, switching places at dizzying speed as she ran the program again, and still nothing happened.

"Wait." Tom grasped her upper arms. "What was that thing he said? It wasn't the numbers, it was the relationship between them?"

"Yes. Oh. . . yes!" Natasha breathed. Her hands flew over the keyboard again, this time figuring out how many numbers stood between 17 and 24. . . 24 and 13. . . 13 and 36. . . . There was always a right answer, if you could just make it through all the calculations. That was what she loved so much about math. In a matter of minutes she had created all the possible combinations of the numbers Fenster had played and determined the intervals between them. . . and she fed those numbers back into the program.

The computer whirred for what seemed like an aeon. Tom leaned in close to Natasha, peering at the screen past the ghostly reflected images of the two of them, praying at the altar of Macintosh for their numbers to come up.

Suddenly the computer gave a different beep and flashed its screen at them.

Welcome to Banco Mundial, it said. *Please enter your password.*

Piece of cake: that had been given to them already, by another operative. Within moments they were elbow deep in Loki's money, freezing every one of his accounts so that his ill-gotten funds would be of absolutely no use to him.

It was such a quiet victory: no explosions, no gun battles, no helicopters, no handcuffs. Loki was nowhere nearby, yet Tom and Natasha had trapped him as surely as if they had him in leg irons. Because without his billions, Loki was helpless. The blinking cursor on the computer screen signaled his downfall.

"It is done," Natasha said quietly.

"Nice work," Tom responded. They glanced at each other, both understanding this was no time to rest on their laurels. Time was of the essence: they had to get back to New York to see how this would affect Loki in person. With the practiced expertise of two agents always on the go, they quickly packed their bags and left the room as pristine and empty of clues as they had found it.

Hell, they even remembered to tip the chambermaid.

HERE WERE SOME THINGS THAT ED

Unused Shoes

Fargo noticed as he strolled—strolled!—through the West Village on a beautiful afternoon. First of all, for two years he'd viewed everyone at crotch level, and it was really nice to be up and out of a wheelchair. Second of all, since his operation he had been so nervous about his crutches that he'd spent most of his time looking down, so while he had an intimate knowledge of the intricate patterns of his suede Vans, he had absolutely no clue what was going on in the neighborhood that had been home to him all his life.

So: First of all, the scaffolding was gone from the garden-enclosed library on Sixth Avenue. And the grime was already beginning to resettle on the brown bricks.

Second, there was a brand-new J. Crew where the store that sold wigs, sequins, and size-sixteen stilettos to drag queens used to be.

Third, it turned out that the annoying traffic cop that used to tower over Ed was only about five-foot-two.

It was amazing what came into view when you had your body back. He hadn't lost his eyesight, but the world looked totally new to Ed, anyway.

Another revelation was just how difficult it was. Walking was hard work! At least, it was when your muscles were used to having some backup. But he was extremely pleased to feel them ache because it meant they were getting stronger by the second. Shinsplints—that was sweet.

Yet even as he maneuvered from corner to corner, Ed felt another weird feeling creeping up his spine and into his consciousness. A feeling that was definitely different from the joy, pride, and triumph that pervaded the forefront of his mind. What was it. . . was he feeling. . . guilty?

Yeah! That was it. He felt totally and completely guilty. He'd hoped for so long that he'd get the use of his legs back, and he was painfully aware that most of the people he'd been with in physical therapy were definitely not enjoying a late afternoon stroll right at this minute. And he felt like he was sort of betraying every last one of them.

As if she'd been sent by some external form of his conscience, a girl appeared out of the crowd, humming her way down the sidewalk in a motorized wheelchair. The throngs of midday pedestrians kept getting in her way, and a massive crack in the sidewalk was not helping matters. As one wheel caught, she leaned over, muttering and cursing at the useless chair she was in.

"Here, let me help," Ed said, stepping forward to give the chair a shove.

"No, thanks, Boy Scout," she snapped, slapping his

hand away. "I can handle this myself. Don't bother."

"Hey!" Ed said, genuinely hurt. "I was just. . ."

"Well, don't," she said. "See? I got it. Now back off."

She ran over his foot with her right wheel as she—well, she would have been stalking off if she were on two legs. The chair made it kind of hard for her to finesse an indignant exit, but she was doing her best. The back of her head gave off a distinct aura of hostility as she headed downtown.

Ed wanted to say something. But what? "Hey, I used to be in one of those, but medical science did me right!" Yes, Infomercial Ed would surely crack her exterior. "Don't be mad at me—I'm not like everyone else on the street!" *No, I'm twice as annoying because I know how you feel, yet I still have full use of my legs.*

Nope. There was not a word he could say that would make a difference. And as he watched her bumping down the sidewalk away from him, Ed could discern one more emotion bubbling around in his consciousness: relief. Complete relief that he was not in that girl's unused shoes.

Everything
went black,
and then red
tendrils
crept like
wiggling
worms
across her
field of
vision.

blow

by

blow

POOM.

Gaia hit the floor with as much grace as a flounder landing on the deck of a fishing boat. She didn't even bother jumping up. She couldn't believe she'd been taken so completely by surprise by a girl half her size and with a quarter of her muscle.

Civics Lesson

She was lying on her back, staring at the ceiling, trying to put together what had just happened, when Tatiana's angry face loomed into her vision.

"Do you want another one?" Tatiana asked uncertainly. "Or are you going to keep your stupid accusations to yourself?"

Gaia was pretty sure she didn't want any more of what Tatiana was dishing out. And she had to admit, that had been a pretty good shot. Lightning reflexes were no match for an angry Russian girl defending her mother, apparently.

"No, thank you," Gaia said "I'll take option B."

"Good." Tatiana relaxed a little, looking a bit relieved, even shocked at her own actions. She flexed her left hand, massaging it with her right, and grimaced in pain.

"You have to be careful when you hit someone with a fist," Gaia said helpfully, sitting up and scrooching a few feet away from Tatiana on the floor. "You didn't have your thumb inside your fist, did you?"

122

"I don't think so," Tatiana said, glaring down at her hurt hand. "Mostly I think I bruised my knuckles on your very hard head."

"Good, because if you put your thumb inside your fist, you'd probably break it. And you're right. My head is pretty hard sometimes. Big mouth, hard head."

"Yes. Well." Tatiana sat on the floor and leaned against the wall, facing Gaia. "If I am going to be completely honest, I have to tell you that I have often suspected my mother of being some kind of agent. She is extremely secretive. When I was a small child, I would accept her explanations, but these days it's a bit difficult. Her stories are a bit—lame. I mean, why would an exporter of Oriental rugs need her on a plane at three in the morning? Or require her to carry a gun?"

"Okay, now, see?" Gaia exclaimed, throwing her hands in the air. "The gun is really the kicker."

"But no! I do not take it this far," Tatiana objected. "Whatever she is doing, it is not evil, and it does not hurt people. You do not know my mother. She has helped more people than you will ever know. I have seen her sacrifice her own happiness time and again to make sure others are safe."

Gaia sighed. "I can think of a million cases in the history books—and the newspapers—where someone who seemed like a saint turned out to be more of a devil. But I understand that you'd be crazy to accept what I'm saying at face value."

"Listen to me, you do not understand," Tatiana told her. "Before I was born, my mother—do you know this word, *refuseniks?*"

Gaia was aware that the average teenager would probably think the refuseniks were a garage band from Portland, but she knew the real deal: Back when Russia was still the Soviet Union, they'd refused their citizens the right to move out of the country—and made their lives hell while doing it.

"Yes, I know that word," she said.

"My mother worked to help these people escape. Very hard, this job. Very dangerous. The state at the time was oppressive, and you want to talk about double-crossing snakes? They were everywhere. Someone would turn you in for a week's supply of bread and a bottle of vodka."

"Yeah, but that doesn't mean—"

"And do you know about the Russian Mafia?" Tatiana went on.

Gaia sighed. Maybe Tatiana was beginning to grow on her, but did that mean Gaia had to put up with this little civics lesson?

"These are horribly dangerous men," Tatiana told her. "They make your godfather, Marlon Brando, look like a pussycat. My mother stood up to them in

Moscow and barely escaped with her life. It is one of the reasons we are here now."

"The other reason being my dad," Gaia pointed out.

"Perhaps. Or perhaps he is just making the move much easier for my mother. Either way, even here she must be very careful." She sighed. "That was the reason she gave me for the gun. But I still always wondered."

"I found letters between them," Gaia said. "They seem pretty convincing, but I have evidence that they have to be lies."

"Well, I found a postcard that your father sent to my mother. He obviously trusts her. Are you saying that your father's a fool?"

"I would never say something like that about my father. But he doesn't have the evidence I have. I'm operating off a tip I got straight from a CIA agent," Gaia finally admitted.

"Interesting," Tatiana said. "And this 'evidence' is. . . ?"

"Well." Gaia paused. "Well, I don't know exactly. But George seemed very sure."

"Uh-huh."

"Listen, George has already proved himself to be trustworthy. He used to be my guardian before he. . . oh."

"Yes?"

"Well, he sort of had this wife who turned out to be a double agent, too."

"So he's not a particularly good judge of character," Tatiana said.

"Look, I trust George," Gaia said flatly, though she couldn't deny that Tatiana was making some excellent points. "If he says he has evidence, then he just does."

""Well, I would be very interested in meeting this agent for myself," Tatiana said, sitting back and give Gaia a determined glare. "If he is saying my mother is making love to a man only to destroy him, I would like him to say it to my face. I must see this evidence for myself. From the horse's hoof, as you say."

"Mouth."

"What?"

"The horse's mouth. You want to hear it from the horse's mouth."

"Yes. I want to hear this talking horse tell me what proof there is of this accusation."

Gaia stood, shaking her legs to get the pins and needles out of them. She shook her head. "You are *so* not meeting this guy. Trust me, he knows what he's talking about."

That clinched it. "You are wrong. I am *so* so meeting this guy," Tatiana informed her.

Gaia was about to object again when something caught her eye out the window. "What the. . ."

"What is it?"

"There's some guy out there messing with a lady," Gaia said. As if in response, a bloodcurdling shriek blasted from the street below, followed by a wail of complete and total helpless misery.

The George conundrum was going to have to wait.

THE COUNTRYSIDE WHIZZED PAST

The Hazy Distance

Tom at an alarming rate as he raced through it on the saddle of a borrowed Harley. It was a little macho, maybe even smacking of a slight midlife crisis, but there was no denying that it was the quickest way to get from point A (the resort) to point B (the airport).

They had frozen Loki's assets. Now they had to get the hell out of Dodge. Once Loki found out what Tom had done, he would strike where he was most vulnerable: Gaia. It killed Tom not to be close enough to protect her. On a normal day, Loki was dangerous. When threatened, the danger factor was raised exponentially.

The 500 ccs of power hummed beneath his saddle while Natasha held on around his waist. He veered down every back road imaginable, finally seeing the airport in the hazy distance. There was a back entrance that he remembered from a long-ago assignment here, and he shot for it, hoping against hope it hadn't been fenced in.

It hadn't. All was well as he buzzed across the wide tarmac, heading for the chartered plane parked at a short distance from the tiny airport. The gangway was lowered; the pilot was already aboard: All was ready to get him out of this country and back to New York.

He pulled the bike up short, allowed Natasha to hop off the back, and stepped off, throwing down the kickstand and yanking off his helmet in one fluid motion.

"Nick!" he shouted up to the pilot, an old friend from other operations. "Are you going to get me the hell out of this godforsaken paradise?"

"Before you can say 'piña colada,'" Nick responded. "Now, get your sorry ass up here before I have to take off without you."

Tom was halfway up the gangway, and Natasha was already strapped into her seat, when his cell phone rang. "Go," he told her.

"Tom, it's George," he heard. "Did I catch you in time?"

"In time for what? We're taxiing down the runway in about eight seconds," Tom said.

"Stop! Don't leave the island," George insisted. His voice held a desperate urgency. "Loki is there. He found out what you were doing and where you are,

and he's on the island now. You can't leave there—
you've got to neutralize him first."

"What?" He grabbed Nick's arm, stopping him
from pulling the air lock closed. "Loki is here?"

Natasha leapt from her seat, already prepared for
the change of plans.

"He's there," George repeated. "At the estate on the
south fork of the island—I've sent the address to your
Blackberry."

Tom looked at the e-mail and noted the location.

"What about Gaia?" Tom asked. "Please tell me
she's still okay. George?"

But the phone was cutting out. He could only
make out every other word George was saying.

"George! Is Gaia safe?"

The phone's connection was failing. The last thing
he heard was George saying, "Good-bye, old friend.
Just go."

Something felt wrong. Very wrong. There must have
been a leak the size of the Holland Tunnel within the
operation. How could Loki have found him so quickly?

"We've got to go," he said. "Or I should say, I have
to go. Natasha, Nick can take you back to New York
right now."

"Nick can take himself back to New York," Natasha
responded. "I'm going with you."

Tom's nagging misgivings were shoved unceremo-
niously to the back of his mind. He had no time to

wonder what was going on. He was an agent, and it was time to follow instructions. And never had he so looked forward to an assignment. Neutralize Loki? The phrase sounded so neat and polite. As he fired up the Harley again and peeled out on the tarmac, Tom could practically feel his brother's throat beneath his ever-tightening fingers.

HEATHER TRIED TO ACT LIKE SHE

The Blue Pill

was already fearless as she climbed the wide, wooden stairs, but she wasn't having too much luck. She was a city girl, and she had certain instincts. Instincts that reminded her to walk in the street rather than inside an enclosed underpass—better to be hit by a car than lose her wallet to a mugger. Instincts that made her stay within sight of the token-booth operator and spot the conductor's car if she were taking the subway at night. Instincts that told her never to take a friendly ride, even from a cop. And instincts that were wary of the outer-borough address and absolutely desolate location of this abandoned warehouse.

She was in Queens, for God's sake. Long Island

City. As if there could be a less trendy address within the five boroughs. This was where fashion victims came to die, it seemed.

The place even smelled dangerous. Like it hadn't been mopped since time began. If a marauding pack of homeless gang members didn't get her, the Ebola virus probably would.

Still, when Josh squeezed her hand and turned to smile at her, Heather felt her body ooze with reassurance, as if his gaze were filled with warm wax, pouring into her insides. She squeezed back and smiled in a way that, she hoped, at least successfully faked some confidence.

When they got to the third floor, Josh unhooked a massive sliding door, yanking it sideways so that it whined in protest, gray paint flaking onto the concrete floor. Inside, it was a whole other story.

She stepped into a long, wide room, as big as a city block, the walls stripped to bare brick and hung with large and weird oil paintings. The floor was a freshly sanded wood that gleamed with a recent coat of wax. A friendly kitchen stood out in stark white to her left, and the only interruption to the flow of the room was a white raised loft off in the corner. It was, in a word, stunning.

"What a great place to throw a New Year's Eve party," she said. "I don't suppose I could rent this out?"

"Heather," Josh said, ignoring her insouciant question. "I want you to meet Oliver. Gaia's father."

Heather turned to face this mysterious man.

"I wish I could say it was a pleasure," she said, sizing him up. "But I can't exactly say Gaia and I are best buddies."

Wow. For an old guy he was kind of. . . dashing? Was that the word? Heather usually didn't go in for dinosaurs. That said, this guy was cool looking. He was in great shape, for one thing. He had to be at least forty-five, but she could tell his athletic, lanky frame was flawless. And he was dressed impeccably, in a custom-tailored Brooks Brothers suit. His hair was reddish blond, just enough to give his face an aura of brightness, and his deep-set eyes were the most reassuring liquid blue.

In short, Gaia's dad was a major babe.

"Well, it's certainly my pleasure to meet you," he said, gazing intently into her eyes with a look that clearly said, "You are the only person on this planet at this moment." He shook her hand with a two-handed grip and gave her a sincere, knowing nod. "I'm aware that Gaia can be difficult. It is one of the more tragic chapters in my life, the fact that I can't repair my relationship with her. I hope she hasn't caused you too much discomfort."

So Heather wasn't the only one who'd had more than a fair share of Gaia trouble. She'd turned her back on her own damn father. Heather shook her head, wondering at the many people Gaia had shit on in her life. It never occurred to her not to believe everything he was saying to her. It never occurred to her that Gaia might have excellent reason to detest the man who claimed to be her father.

Meanwhile, Heather felt self-conscious. This guy was so much cooler than she'd thought he was going to be! She'd expected some kind of weird, bald mad scientist. But apart from her greedy need for the fearless injection, all of a sudden Heather genuinely wanted to make this charismatic man happy. "No worries," she said. "I mean, I can handle Gaia, no problem. She's not so bad."

He smiled gratefully, as if he knew she was fibbing on his account, and let go of her hand. It suddenly felt cold and lonely outside of his grip.

"I can see where Gaia gets her looks from, anyway," Heather added, then recoiled at how stupid that sounded.

"That's kind of you, thank you," Oliver said. "But Gaia really resembles her mother."

"So, uh... are we going to do this?" Josh interrupted.

"Of course. Heather, won't you come in? Have a seat at the table here? Would you like something to drink—a Diet Coke or something?" Oliver asked.

"No, that's all right," Heather said, sitting at a large oak table that had a big metal suitcase sitting on top of it. "I'm really looking forward to this. I've been taking the pills that Josh gave me, and I am really, really ready to go through with this."

"I wanted to make sure that was the case," Oliver said. He took the seat next to her. "There's no turning back from this. And I don't think you've ever had to make a decision this serious in your life. It's a bigger commitment than a short haircut or a tattoo," Oliver said with a smile. "Like when Keanu Reeves chooses the blue pill in *The Matrix*. Except this is not a movie. This is your life. Do you understand what we're undertaking?"

"You underestimate me," Heather responded, looking deeply into the older man's eyes. "There's no need to call up some pop-culture reference to soften me up. I'm not your average high-school girl."

"That's what I thought," Oliver said. "I'm glad my feeling about you was correct. Josh," he said, glancing across the room, "everything you said about her was true."

Heather flushed with pride as she beamed at Josh. Oddly, his smile back at her was a bit uncertain.

"Why don't you take a moment, go to the ladies' room if you like," Oliver said. "It'll take me a few minutes to get the injection ready." He opened the big metal suitcase, and Heather blanched at the sight of a bunch of glass bottles and a hypodermic needle so big, it could have been a tube of toothpaste.

Josh brought her to the other end of the loft and showed her to a little alcove where the bathroom was.

"Hey," he said, taking her by the arm before she could enter. "It's not too late to change your mind."

"Josh," Heather said. "Is this another one of your little tests? Because I'm really not in the mood."

"Actually, this is just me being your boyfriend and making sure you're okay with all this."

"Well, stop," Heather said.

"You're right." Josh gave her a nod. "I'm sorry. Go ahead, I'll be waiting for you here."

Heather paused, finally giving him a reassuring smile. "That's all right," she told him. "I'm glad you care enough to check up on me. But really, you should just be happy for me."

"I am," Josh said. He gave her a peck on the cheek, and he stepped aside and let her go into the bathroom.

Inside, she studied herself in the dim glow of the pinkish lightbulbs. *So long, wimpy girl,* she thought. *And hello, warrior princess.*

"All right, boys," she called as she stepped back into the loft. "Let's do this." She strode over to the table and held out the soft white expanse of her inner arm.

Oliver smiled indulgently. "That's very nice," he said. "But I need an area with a little more. . . muscle."

"Oh! You mean my. . . Oh!" Heather blushed. "Well, whatever floats your boat," she said teasingly, and turned around.

135

"If you wouldn't mind?" he asked.

"I usually get dinner and a movie first," she joked, then unbuttoned her jeans and lowered them so the top half of her butt was exposed.

"Just a moment now," Oliver's voice floated from behind her.

Heather's face burned with embarrassment, but she placed her hands firmly on the table, gripping its sides with nervousness. Josh was facing her, sitting on an overstuffed chair and watching intently. It was hard to read his expression, but she smiled reassuringly.

Then she felt a fiery sting that lit up her whole right side. Her body gave a jolt, and for a moment she could see absolutely nothing.

"Oh, *ow!*" she yelped.

And then the most extraordinary feeling shot through her, like a lightning bolt but weirder. Everything went black, and then red tendrils crept like wiggling worms across her field of vision. It was sort of like what she saw when she pressed her fingers against her closed eyes—fantastic swirls of color and light—but everything was moving so much more quickly. And the feeling? Pure adrenaline. She imagined this was what bungee jumping would feel like. It was as if she'd been shoved off the top of a building and she was falling, except instead of terror she felt only excitement—excitement, pleasure, euphoria, but no fear. No fear at all.

The fantastic shadows parted, and she was suddenly aware of the hard surface of the wooden table beneath her hands. And of the fact that she hadn't taken a breath in almost a minute. She gave a loud gasp, snapping back into the present, and then heard a long, throaty laugh erupt from her mouth.

"Whoa," was all she could say. Her vision cleared, and the first thing that floated into her consciousness was Josh's gorgeous face, his forehead creased with worry.

"Heather?" she heard him say.

"Mmm. Yes?" she answered, floating in a haze of endorphins.

"Wait. No!" he said.

Heather heard an odd click, then felt pressure at her temple: cool, hard steel. From his spot behind her, Oliver had put down his needle—and was holding a gun to Heather's head. She'd seen enough episodes of "Law & Order" to know what was happening. The safety was off, and he was ready to splatter her brains all over the freshly finished hardwood floor.

It must be nice to feel sure of something. There are some truths that are absolute: hot and cold, for instance. But beyond physical sensations, I'm never sure of anything anymore.

Unlike Tatiana. She is so convinced that her mother is good. And that must feel nice, even though it's only a delusion. I almost feel bad, forcing her to see the truth. But would I be doing her any kind of favor by letting her live in a dreamworld? No way. She's got to wake up and smell the garbage, just like I did.

There's nothing sure in this world. Not even your parents. The sooner she realizes that, the better. I don't even know who my father is, let alone if he's good or evil. So if she finds out her mother is definitely a baddie, well, she's one step ahead of me.

All right. Is it time for thirty seconds of truth? I'll admit something to you. Yeah, I've got it in for Natasha because George said she's trouble. Yeah, I have a problem with Tatiana's flirtatious relationship with Ed. But if you really want to talk about why I can't stand being around these two, I suppose a shrink might tell you it's because it brings up some long-ago feelings in me.

Feelings I'd thought I crushed out of existence after my mother died.

The fact is, I can remember my mother's smell, the feeling of her hair, the way her old jeans were so soft when I put my head in her lap. If she were alive today, I don't know if I'd be the kind of daughter who told her everything and asked her advice. I don't know if we'd fight about my curfew. I don't know if she'd yank me into line and give me lectures about living up to my potential at school. But I do know I'd love her so much. I do know I'd defend her to the death. I do know that if someone said boo about her, I'd punch her in the head, too.

I wish I had someone I loved
that much.

Damn it.

I almost wish I was wrong
about Natasha. I wish that bitch
wasn't a government agent, working for Loki. Because when
Tatiana learns the truth, it's
going to break her heart. And
she'll be just another girl like
me, a motherless freak with no
one to count on.

Now, is that fair? No. And I
wish with all my heart that it
just wasn't so.

Grown-ups suck.

The plane's taking off. And instead of being on board, I'm back on this bike with Tom.

I know he got the word from George, but I can't help thinking something is wrong.

I've been through a lot in this life. There were times, when Russia was still the Soviet Union, when I wasn't sure I'd survive to adulthood. Crammed into that disgusting apartment in Moscow with my entire family, waiting on lines for hours just for a loaf of bread. Watching my father being taken away by the secret police because of sus- pected antigovernment activity. And the black-market hoodlums, who were just as dangerous to us. All I wanted was to grow up.

And then I did. Tatiana's father vanished just before she was born, and I was alone in that squalid hospital, giving birth without anesthetic, with a doctor who had all the empa- thy of an army sergeant, barking

at me to stop wailing, I was
giving her a headache because I
thought I was going to die that
day. And in the weeks afterward, when I suffered from a
horrible infection and nearly
died, I actually prayed for
death, the pain was so bad. But
I survived it. I survived that
illness, I survived my child-
hood, I survived losing everyone that meant anything to me,
one by one. And I swore that
was the last time I'd be forced
by circumstance to endure pain
I had no control over. If I was
going to live my life constantly fighting battles, at
least they would be battles I
would pick. I wouldn't cower
anymore. I contacted a friend
who knew someone who knew someone else—that is how everything
is done in Russia—and finally
joined up with the American
agency. I began my life as a
spy.

It felt very good, to fight
against the powers that oppressed

me. And after communism fell, I continued to do this work, because there is always evil in the world.

It felt good. But it never felt wonderful.

This feels wonderful. This man makes me feel clever, beautiful, accomplished. Working with him makes me my best self. He is like a drug. A good drug, but a drug that I must have. I am not sure about that plane, taking off behind me. I have misgivings about where we are going on this motorcycle. But God help me, I cannot let go. All I can do is stick with him and hang on for dear life.

He looked remarkably like Bugs Bunny, in that one cartoon where his plane's **when** going **worlds** down and he sort **collide** of melts into the pilot's chair—with his hands clutching the armrests.

ON THE STREET BELOW, GAIA AND

Tatiana could see a woman screaming as someone took off with her child.

Snot-Nose Incident

"Have your secretary call mine," Gaia said, already halfway out the door. "We'll finish this discussion later."

"Oh, no, you don't!" Tatiana grabbed her keys and a jacket and followed close behind Gaia. "I'm not leaving you alone until you take me to this CIA man. Do you hear me, Gaia? I am coming with you!"

There was no sense in trying to reason with Tatiana, Gaia thought. Anyway, she'd never be able to keep up. Gaia took the stairs five and six at a time, taking whole landings in a leap. Behind her, Tatiana's feet drummed down the same stairs. They burst out on the street and followed the woman's trembling finger.

Gaia took off first, but she hadn't counted on Tatiana's speed. The Village School didn't have a track team, but back in Russia she had actually trained with the Olympic track-and-field team. She was a runner—a sprinter, in fact, and despite Gaia's almost superhuman pace, Tatiana was able to keep up with her easily.

And they both closed in on the baby-snatching creep without too much trouble. The guy must have been desperate, committing such a high-profile crime. And dumb, too. He was headed for Central Park.

They chased him into an entrance, and he immediately headed downtown, leaping over bushes and walls. Finally there was only one place he could go: He leapt, with the child still crammed under his arm, right into the polar bear's habitat.

Now, Tatiana hadn't been in New York long, but she knew you weren't supposed to get anywhere near the polar bears. They looked big, cute, and gentle, and it was fun to stand outside the partition as they swam around in their moat, holding your hand against the glass and marveling at how much bigger their paws were. Word had it that ten years earlier, some stupid kids had climbed into their lair in the middle of the night and got turned into bear chow in two seconds flat. It was no joke: They were wild animals.

Tatiana stopped short, her heart in her throat, but Gaia never even paused. Her eyes flashed as if she were calculating something at top speed, and she looked around quickly, taking in her surroundings with the efficiency of a computer scanner. In a second she had grabbed a length of hose lying nearby— probably to give the bears a shower—and tied it firmly to a metal pole, letting the other end dangle down into the bears' habitat. And then she leapt down, as casually as if she were jumping a hurdle in gym class.

The polar bears weren't like cats, Tatiana noticed. They didn't circle their prey casually. They were loping toward the guy with the kid quickly, and he was frozen in shock.

"I wouldn't go there, bears," Gaia shouted, conking one of them on the head with a rock to get his attention. "Eating a human is a capital offense—even if he's just a child-molesting creep!"

The bears changed direction, heading straight for Gaia, but she was way ahead of them. She leapt from her craggy rock to the one that hung over the kidnapper and grabbed the kid right out of his hands. She shoved the man over the divider into the monkey cage, then ran back, with the child now firmly held under her arm, to where the dangling hose was. Any moment of hesitation would definitely cost her life—but that human hesitation was uncannily absent. Tatiana couldn't believe what she was seeing.

She yanked the hose to pull Gaia up and out of the bears' den, and all three of them collapsed on the hard ground. Now, finally, they could see that the little girl was a gorgeous, blue-eyed two-year-old. She looked first at Gaia, then at Tatiana, and then broke into a heart-rending wail. Gaia was closest to her—plus she had just saved her from the bear—so the poor kid grabbed her around the neck, mistaking her for someone who possessed even a shred of a nurturing instinct.

"Hey! Oh. Hey, come on," Gaia said, suddenly looking nervous. "Um. Don't cry." She was positively wooden.

"Give her a hug," Tatiana said. "Come on, Gaia, she's scared!" She tried to rub the little girl's back, but for some unknown reason, it was Gaia she wanted comfort from.

Gaia put her arms around the child as if she was hugging a porcupine. She patted her little head awkwardly. "Hey, stop that. It's really loud."

"Gaia!" Tatiana started laughing. "You're hopeless." She took the little girl's chubby hands from around Gaia's neck and enveloped her in a reassuring embrace, feeling the child's trembling body latch onto hers for dear life. It was such a natural thing to do—yet it was completely beyond Gaia's grasp.

"There, there," she said, giving Gaia a wry grin as she shook her head. Gaia seemed a little out of it, but she rallied after a moment or two. "Come on," Tatiana told her. "I think I hear the police."

They stood, and Tatiana carried the little girl out to the pathway, where several officers and the girl's mother were at a standstill, not knowing where the kidnapper had run.

"Sophie!" the mom yelped, and the little girl flung

herself into her arms. "Thank you so much," she told Tatiana, who shoved Gaia forward.

"Oh, this is your hero," she said.

"Whatever. If you want the creep who did this, he's in the monkey moat." Gaia shrugged. They could hear his shrieks as he was overrun by the wild primates. Tatiana had heard they could break a grown man's arm. It sounded like they were trying, anyway.

The officers ran off to nab their guy, with two remaining behind to get Sophie and her mother home safely. Which made it easy for Gaia and Tatiana to melt back into the shadows and cross diagonally toward Fifty-ninth Street and the south end of the park.

"I wonder how come a girl who's not afraid of polar bears is frightened to death by a crying child?" Tatiana teased, still amused at Gaia's sudden change of mood.

"Guess that's just another mystery of life," Gaia said.

"Well, then let's clear up our earlier mystery," Tatiana told her. "I would like to speak to this man who says such terrible things about my mother."

Gaia groaned. "Tatiana, I appreciate your help with that little snot-nose incident—really, your contribution was invaluable—but I don't think you want to get involved in this situation, and I am not bringing you downtown."

"You are so stubborn," Tatiana said. Anger flashed into her eyes again. "For God's sake, Gaia. Forget the child you just saved. That is not why I am asking. I need to speak to this person who knows so much about my mother. Or who thinks he does."

"I'll handle it," Gaia said. "I'll get the information from him and fill you in."

"You will forgive me for not believing you completely when you say that," Tatiana said. "You are not the most dependable person in general, if you have not noticed."

Gaia gritted her teeth. Part of her wouldn't have minded having someone at her side when she confronted George. But the images flashed through her head: Sam. Mary. Her mother. Even Ella. Gaia's past was littered with friends who got involved—and paid the price.

"No." Her answer was flat and final. But it was not a word Tatiana liked hearing—especially not in this particular case.

"Gaia, listen to me," Tatiana said. "Tonight has been a little strange. I found out my mother is dating someone. For anyone normal, that would be traumatic, but then you tell me she is some sort of spy. I begin to think about her habits, and I know she has been lying to me about something. But my instincts tell me you are still wrong about her. Gaia, she is all I have in this world, and I need to know the truth. Why must you stand between me and the information I need?"

"Because it's too risky," Gaia said. "This isn't an episode of 'Scooby Doo.' You could really get killed."

Tatiana paused, considering for a moment. "Perhaps my mother will get killed if I don't do something," she said. Then she shifted her tone, trying to lighten things up a bit. "Besides, I didn't get killed by the giant polar bear. And I saved you from the terrible task of being thanked for saving that child."

Gaia laughed in spite of herself. She could feel her resolve weakening. Tatiana was so determined, and Gaia of all people could appreciate where that determination was coming from. Plus Gaia was lonely.

"Don't you have something better to do?" she asked halfheartedly. "Like go see your boyfriend, Ed?"

Tatiana's face froze in a tight smile. "Ed is most certainly not my boyfriend."

Gaia regarded Tatiana with renewed interest. Ed had stopped calling, huh? So Tatiana was going through the same Ed withdrawal she was. Jealous as she felt about Tatiana's flirting, Gaia couldn't find it in her heart to rub it in—it was too understandable. Besides, the girl looked so stricken. Like a little deer.

"All right, all right, I'll tell you what." Gaia took

Tatiana by the elbow and led her to the south end of the park, toward the N train. "If you'll stop looking so sad, I'll take you to talk to my connection."

"I knew you would see it my way," Tatiana told her, peering intently at her as they walked along.

"What are you looking at?" Gaia asked.

"I never saw you act human before," Tatiana said. "I'm trying to get used to it."

"Well, there's no need for that," Gaia told her, patting her pockets in search of her MetroCard. "Believe me, it's not something I do too often."

BENT OVER THE WOODEN TABLE,

Ugh! Fear!

her butt still stinging from the injection and with the cold hard steel of a major firearm pressed to her temple, Heather was definitely treading in some new territory. Yet she wasn't scared. Her mind calculated the entire situation with smooth precision: *This guy could kill me right now. I don't want to die today. If I do nothing, he can kill me, and if I try to do something, he might not. So I'd better do something now.*

As soon as the thought was complete, Heather reached up with her right hand and jerked the barrel of the gun up toward the roof. She twisted around so she had some leverage, and before Oliver could object, she was on her back with her arm straight up, holding the gun in Oliver's hand well away from her head. It fired into the air, leaving a dent the size of a fist in the brick wall.

"Hey, Doctor, that's not a hypodermic needle," she said.

"And that's not your head," Oliver responded, nodding toward the pulverized brick of the wall.

"Fancy that," Heather said, and laughed. "I think you've proved your point. May I let go of this gun now, or are you going to destroy me before you have a chance to see what I can do?"

Oliver opened his hand so that the gun hung loosely from his index finger. "Experiment ended," he said, giving her a knowing smile. "Subject seems to possess an absolute lack of fear."

"Subject is fearless," she said, letting go of the gun. She sat up slowly, warily, a smile still playing across her face. She knew she should be cautious, just in case. But scared? She didn't feel a twinge.

"So if you aren't afraid, why did you defend yourself?" Oliver asked.

"I don't want to die," Heather told him. "It was pure self-preservation. I saw there was a threat and acted on it, and defended myself more efficiently than I would have if I'd been all startled and terrified, if I do say so myself."

"God, Oliver," Josh said in a wavery voice.

Only then did Heather turn around to see her superhot savior plastered against the back of his chair. Heather thought he looked remarkably like Bugs Bunny, in that one cartoon where his plane is going down and he sort of melts into the pilot's chair—with his hands clutching the armrests. Josh's eyes were wide with shock, and he had actually broken out into a sweat.

"Heather, are you all right?" he asked.

"I'm better than I've ever been," Heather said. "You don't look so hot, though."

"Indeed, Josh," Oliver said. "Is anything wrong?"

Heather saw Josh's expression change. His concern faded and was replaced by—ugh! Fear! He was *afraid* of Oliver. Heather's opinion of her boyfriend dropped a few notches. All of a sudden he seemed a little wimpy.

She looked back at Oliver, who was regarding her with a satisfied smile. Josh might be freaked out, but this guy was clearly proud of her—and of what he'd done to her. Heather felt satisfied and content, as if someone had flicked on a switch inside her and she was now working better. She felt good. Because an awful lot of things seemed to go along with fear. Anxiety about the AP biology exam? That was gone, replaced by a cool-as-a-cucumber assessment of how much she needed to study, with no ohmigod-I-can't-do-this freak-outs to interrupt her progress. The desperate need for control that had led her sister to starve herself almost to death? Heather could see that was fear, too—and she'd never fall victim to it now.

What she had now was the ultimate power. And she planned to use it—to the absolute limit of her imagination.

THE MANSION WAS EASY ENOUGH TO

find. After tooling around through the impoverished tin shacks that dotted the landscape outside of the resort area, Tom could see the gleaming white structure from miles away. And in a stroke of luck, it sat at the bottom of a long hill, so he could cut the purring Harley engine and coast right up to it in complete silence.

Shark on the Sand

It was magnificent. Blew the hotel away, in fact. Resorts were built with the public in mind, but this mansion was clearly designed for total and complete privacy and to very specific—and fine— taste. Luminous white columns stood out against the gleaming sapphire of the water and the elegant beige sand. Smooth grass, meticulously manicured, gave way to the beach in the distance. But all Tom saw was evil. He had to get inside and find Loki. This was the culmination of years of bitter rivalry, and it was all about to pay off.

Without a word, he and Natasha looked at each other and agreed on a plan. Of course they couldn't go charging into the inner sanctum of their enemy. They would first make a reconnaissance trip, each taking a side of the building, looking for any breach of security that would allow them to enter, and meet back at the bike to debrief. It was standard procedure. And the rules and regulations of the Agency were designed for moments like this—moments that required absolute silence and secrecy.

With practiced movements Tom snuck around his side of the mansion, moving quietly through the thickets of scrubby shrubs and trees that protected the area from the prying eyes of locals. It was slow going, but patience was a necessary skill, and he had mastered it. Before too long he had made it almost down to the beach, taking an optical inventory of the various security systems, gated entrances, and external cameras that dotted the compound. He made notes of several places where he could cut wires or approach in a blind spot. This was going to be easier than he'd thought. In fact, everything was going remarkably smoothly.

Suddenly his attention was caught by movement on the beach. The architect had really done his work: The columns that made the house look so grand were duplicated here, reaching up to nowhere in a surrealistic nod to the total magnificence of the ocean. Between those columns a young woman was strolling hand in hand with a tall, well-built man. The girl was obviously very young—a teenager—yet her body was as muscled as a professional athlete's. Her blond hair hung almost to her waist. And despite the lush surroundings, she was dressed with total casual ease, in cutoff shorts and a worn red T-shirt.

Her attention was completely focused on the young man, and soon his hand wandered from her hand to her waist, and then both of his hands snaked around her athletic frame to fondle her entire body. She clearly welcomed the attention: leaning back against one of the columns, she guided his hands along her body and then put her own hands on his shoulders, his back, his. . .

It was Gaia. Tom realized it with a shock. Loki had somehow brought Gaia here, and she was being seduced by this filthy-minded dirtbag. Was there no depth to which he would not sink? His innocent daughter—he could see it clear as day: that was her favorite T-shirt, from Jerry's Crab House. Tom was so shocked and horrified, he couldn't look away.

Gaia laughed, pushed the boy away from her, then

ran down toward the beach, the boy following her. He was lean, muscled, with jet black hair—a predator, a shark on the sand instead of in the water. Gaia ran in and out of the surf, reaching down to scoop up water and splashing him. What was she doing here? What lies had Loki told her?

It dawned on him that he had never seen her so carefree. At least, not since she was twelve. Gaia was laughing, playing, frolicking in the sand like a high-school kid who didn't have a care in the world. Despite himself—despite his knowledge that she was in the gravest danger, that this beautiful mansion was nothing but a prison, that her life could end at any moment, that the boy she was running with was using her—despite all of it, he wished, for a fleeting moment, that this were all real and that she could really be as untroubled as she now seemed.

She stopped splashing and stood in the low surf, suddenly quiet as she approached the boy, her red shirt soaked and clinging to her body. She threw her arms around him and wrestled him (expertly, of course) to the sand, then stood over him, one leg on either side of his hips. She leaned over, putting her hands on the sand, and kissed his upturned face, first on each cheek, then deeply on the mouth. Then she lowered her body so she was straddling him—still clothed, but with a writhing action that was all too clear in its intention. . . .

Tom burned with anger. And he knew what he had to do next. Whatever the consequences, he had to protect his daughter.

He stepped out of his shrubbery cover and raced down to the beach. "Gaia!" he called out. "Gaia, get away from him. Get away from him!"

The sand gave way beneath his feet and he stumbled, but Tom kept moving, propelled forward by a parent's protective instinct. Finally he reached her and pulled her up by the arm, yanking her out of the sand and away from the demented horndog who'd been feeling her up.

Only the girl who turned around to face him wasn't Gaia. With a rush of relief and then of horror, he realized he'd been tricked.

She looked like Gaia but was older—some sort of trained assassin playing a part. The boy looked remarkably like Josh, who Tom knew had been killed in New York City weeks earlier. What on earth was going on?

Tom reached for his gun, still secured in its holster, but before he could pull it out, he heard another one being cocked. He froze and felt himself being tackled by an overgrown ape of a man, a steroid-enhanced supersized member of Loki's security force.

He let go of the bait and realized with a flood of regret that he'd been had. Lured to this compound by false information—fakery that he'd been totally blind to because of his obsession with Loki. Someone had gotten the best of him, and he had put Natasha at risk because of it.

Even as he was dragged with tremendous force by four men both bigger and more well armed than he was, Tom's mind began making lightning-fast connections, working backward through the entire previous day. How had this happened? How had he been duped into coming here? Where was the hole in his tiny cadre of trusted sources?

Could it have been Nick, the pilot? He didn't think so; Nick hadn't told him not to leave the islands. Was it Natasha? Possibly—as inconceivable as it seemed, he knew she might have a hand in this. That would certainly explain the mysterious phone call earlier. He needed to figure out exactly when things had gone south, who knew where he was. . . .

Oh, no.

God, no. Was it possible?

The warnings against Natasha. The sudden interest in where Gaia lived. The final phone call, faint but firm in its directive to come to this address, just when he'd been about to leave the Caymans. . .

Tom had been betrayed by the only person he truly trusted. Not by his wife, not as the victim of poor judgment, but as a result of malicious, double-crossing duplicity. After years of risking his life for the Agency, after pulling himself and Tom out of tough spots that threatened both their lives, he had called Tom, told him to come here, and then said what—"Good-bye, old friend"?

There was only one person who could be responsible, and the shock of it shattered Tom's heart in ways he'd never realized it could break.

The deadly blow had come from George Niven.

When I was young and joined the Agency—boy, was I green. I mean, I was more serious than the other students at Columbia, sure; I was more serious than anyone. While they were doing bong hits and arguing over the true meaning of "In-A-Gadda-Da-Vida," I was quietly studying, training, and never mentioning what I wanted my vocation to be. It would have sounded strange in the midst of the groovy seventies to admit I wanted to be a spy. Like saying I'd always dreamed of becoming a piston engine. Completely impossible, and even if it were possible, it was just not done.

Except I did it. And George was the first man I worked with.

He was so unbelievably prescient. I swore at first that he had ESP, he could read my mind. I thought I was so slick, and he broke me down within moments of meeting me: after a quarter hour of conversation about nothing more telling than the weather and

my course requirements, he knew I
had a fear of dogs that I'd
barely overcome. He knew every
chink in my armor.

I hated him for that. It felt
like emotional root canal. I was
laid bare, but in the end it made
me much stronger. Because I had
to root out my weaknesses in
order to conquer them.

I don't know how many times he
saved my life. His own life
seemed to be of no consequence to
him. More than once he made a
decision that was almost guaranteed to kill him and went forward
with it for the greater good. He
was a soldier. He put the
Agency's needs above his own.

And this was the man who
taught me.

When Katia died, I had no one
to turn to. I didn't *want* to turn
to anyone, but George found me,
and instead of berating me for
being weak, he somehow filled me
with the strength to go on living. For Gaia. Even if I couldn't
be with her, even if I had to

make her hate me for her own
good. I had to be out here, pro-
tecting her. Watching over her.
Whatever loss I felt over Katia,
I had to transcend. I had to be
both parents. And I had to do it
from afar. An impossible task.
Except George had a knack for
impossibilities.

I wonder what happened to him?
I wonder what part of his brain
gave in first? And what exactly
it gave in to? You could not
threaten his life; he wouldn't
betray a friend for that. He had
no one; Ella was his last human
connection, besides me. Maybe
losing Ella broke him. Maybe it
all goes back to her betrayal.

Or maybe he allowed her to
betray him because he was already
becoming feeble. And I was too lov-
ing, too in awe of him, to see it.

All I know is, I have lost
George. He's dead to me. He's
dead to himself. And something
tells me he's dead, period, if
not now, then as good as dead.
That he'll be gone before I can

ask him any of these questions.
Something tells me that I'll
never be able to satisfy my
curiosity about his ultimate
betrayal not just of me, but of
Gaia.

No more George.
Damn you, old friend.

If she

did anything

now,

irreparable

both

damage

their

parents

were dog

meat.

THE BROWNSTONE ON PERRY STREET

was just as pretty as it had always been. Even Gaia could see that to an objective observer, it was totally cute and quaint.

Spazziest Moves

"You lived here?" Tatiana asked, echoing her thoughts. "It is much more homely than that big building uptown."

"Homey," Gaia told her. "Homely is, like, ugly. This place looks cozy, I know. But believe me, the time I spent here was anything but comfortable."

"Bad memories," Tatiana agreed. "They can make the Winter Palace look like a tin shack."

Gaia showed her the fire escape, her preferred method of secret entry, and just like old times, she swung herself up with great finesse.

"Why are we going in that way?" Tatiana asked, clearly alarmed by Gaia's perch. "I thought we were going to talk to George. Why can we not just ring the front bell to speak to him?"

"I have a very serious no-front-door policy," Gaia responded. "Whenever possible, I like to take people by surprise. It's an old habit." She shrugged. "Besides, I want to look around a bit before we talk to him. See if I can turn up any hard evidence on my own."

"You're a snoop," Tatiana grumbled.

"Yep." Gaia nodded. "You can go home if you want. If you can't handle it, you know."

"I can handle this!" Tatiana glared up at Gaia. "Just tell me how to get up there. I will do the rest."

Gaia had only been teasing about sending Tatiana home. She was definitely more interesting than Gaia had given her credit for, and her determination was impressive.

Tatiana followed Gaia's directions on where to climb and how to stand so that she could haul her little bod up to the bottom of the fire escape. The structure of the metal scaffolding was sturdy, but like all fire escapes, it consisted of nothing more than widespread slats bolted to the brick. Climb the steps inside a building, and you're well insulated from the knowledge that you're actually standing two, three, four flights in the air. But on a fire escape, there's no such illusion. You're standing out in the air, and if you look down, even though you feel a solid landing beneath your feet, you see the dizzying drop to the ground below. Gaia could see that this was difficult for Tatiana. As they climbed the metal ladder, Gaia reminded her to stay focused on the trip up the outside of the building, but despite Tatiana's superhuman efforts, her eyes kept drifting downward, and her muscles froze in total and complete terror each time that happened.

This was completely foreign to Gaia. It never ceased to amaze her how fear could mess up an easy task, like this climb. She could feel Tatiana's anxiety mounting as they crept up each flight of rusty stairs.

Gaia realized that this was more than nervousness. Tatiana had a real fear of heights. She hoped she could back up her determination on this trip up the building. Gaia knew Tatiana wanted to prove something to her, but she also knew she might have bitten off more brownstone than she could chew.

Once they finally reached the top, Gaia swung out over the dizzying four-story drop to land, with monkeylike ease, on the windowsill outside her former bedroom. It took some serious balance and maneuvering, but it was small potatoes to Gaia. In a matter of moments she had jimmied the lock and slid open the heavy wooden frame.

Once inside, she leaned out and grinned at Tatiana, who was standing, white-knuckled, on the top flight of the fire escape.

"Come on," she said. "See how easy? I swear to you, this is no big deal—I already did the hard part. All you have to do is jump across."

"Yes. I can do it," Tatiana squeaked.

"Sure, you can. So go ahead," Gaia told her. "If you think about it too long, you'll talk yourself out of it."

Tatiana's eyes were practically spinning around in their sockets, she was so scared. She swallowed, locked her gaze onto Gaia's so she wouldn't look down, and stepped gingerly over the railing so that only her left hand, clinging to the cold metal, kept her from tumbling to the sidewalk. On the ground it was a nothing jump. But up here...

She tried to reach across at the same time as she jumped. It was one of the top-five spazziest moves Gaia had ever seen, and sure enough, she missed the window by a mile.

OF COURSE, GAIA HAD ANTICIPATED

Sentimental Appendicitis

Tatiana's clumsiness and had her legs wedged against the radiator inside the window. It was nothing for her to grab Tatiana under the arms and yank her up to safety. Hell, she didn't even realize she was falling until she was already firmly held in Gaia's grasp, so Gaia had a chance to clap a hand over Tatiana's mouth, barely suppressing her hysterical shriek.

"Shut up," Gaia whispered, wrestling Tatiana into

171

submission even as she dangled in the air. "I know you're scared, but you're okay, so lose the skirt."

She waited for Tatiana's body to go limp in agreement and then yanked her through the window. They lay on the floor, Tatiana's breath coming in ragged, panicked gasps, Gaia's as normal as ever. When Tatiana had composed herself, Gaia sat up.

"Can I trust you not to freak out?" she whispered. Tatiana nodded. Gaia stood, silently, and slipped the window shut; then she paused and listened intently to the sounds inside the house. Not even a creak of the building settling. Apparently their little adventure on the fire escape hadn't alerted George to their presence.

Her room was familiar, but it felt like a million years since she'd stepped through that door. George had told her the truth when he asked her to come back here to live—he hadn't touched a thing in here; it was exactly as she'd left it. Hard to believe how much had happened since then. She remembered how George's wife, hootchie Ella, had pulled the wool over the old guy's eyes and made him think she was as innocent as an Olsen twin while the whole time she was feeding information about him to Loki—and trying her best to turn Gaia into daisy fertilizer. Now that she thought about it, Gaia realized that George was probably losing his marbles even then. That was a big screwup for a company man.

But hadn't he sworn to be more careful in the future?

Yeah. But promises were made to be broken—wasn't that the major lesson in Gaia's life?

"Let's roll," she said. "I want to prove to you once and for all that George is telling the truth." She said it as much for herself as for Tatiana. Some stupid, weak voice inside her head was nagging at her. *George is lying,* it said. *Natasha really is in love with your dad. You have a real shot at happiness, you genetic mutant freak.*

That was a voice she absolutely had to shut up. Self-doubt was as bad as fear; it would trip her up if she let it. She had a purpose, forcing George to prove his allegations, and disappointing as the truth was, she had to face it. Any part of her that denied it was just so much sentimental appendicitis. She forced the voice to the back of her mind and steeled herself.

Together she and Tatiana crept down the stairs toward the foyer. As soon as they got there, the doorbell started ringing with an insistent, urgent buzz.

GEORGE PADDED TO THE FRONT DOOR,

Trouble

not even bothering to check through the peephole to see who it was. After years of being a spy, there were certain instincts he could not shake, try as he might to dull them with single-malt scotch: on the other side of that door, his old spy self told him, was trouble.

Besides, the timing was right. He'd made the call to Tom just a few hours ago—the call that had sentenced his old friend to certain death. By now he would have rushed off to his doom instead of getting on the plane. That woman Natasha, too: doomed. Loki was probably here to gloat. To torment George with his betrayal. What he didn't know was that there was no torture worse than George's self-loathing.

His old friend had taken his advice without questioning it. As he should have. Why would he suspect a mole so close? George unlocked the door. It swung open with a mournful creak, revealing Loki.

"You shouldn't have dressed up for me," Loki muttered, taking in the sight before him in disgust.

"Can I offer you a drink?" George asked, closing his flannel robe and knotting its sash, as if that would somehow make up for the fact that he was shuffling around in pajamas and slippers with a three-day growth of gray stubble on his suddenly aged face.

"Of what, some rotgut you had delivered so you could drown your pathetic sorrows in private?" Loki asked, stepping into the hallway with a menacing air that made George take a step backward.

"I only drink single-malt scotch," George muttered. "If I am going to drink myself to death, I insist on doing it in style."

"You truly are pathetic," Loki said, staring George down so that the older man had to look away. He began making a long, slow circuit around him. "Once upon a time, you were a prime operative. More than just dependable. People looked up to you. Even agents who outranked you asked you for advice. George Niven was a name that was synonymous with total and complete honor. But after Ella. . . you lost your edge."

"Don't you lecture me," George shouted, waving his drink at Loki so that the ice clinked. "I did your dirty work. That's all you need. So you can just go away and leave me here."

"And did you do my dirty work properly?" Loki asked, pausing in his circular stroll. "Can you assure me Gaia believed your fallacy?"

George looked down, his disheveled hair and troubled expression suddenly making him look like a sad little boy. "Indeed," he told Loki. "Gaia completely believes that Natasha is an evil agent who's out to destroy her father. I even planted seeds of doubt in *his* mind, I think. It was all too easy. I thought Gaia was smarter than that—but she believed it all."

"Well, then I guess you did do your job—for once," Loki said. "Maybe there's still some fire in the old furnace after all. You've been a great help to me. I appreciate your warning Tom about his lady love, your attempts to seed his doubt in her. And your little phone call to Tom's cell phone was also of great assistance. I have captured him.

He's in my custody, and it's only a matter of time before I destroy him."

George mumbled something that Loki couldn't hear. "What was that, old man?"

"It's no wonder she believed me," George mumbled. "She doesn't know who to trust. We've destroyed her trust—all of us."

Loki was about to respond when a clatter upstairs made his head jerk back. George looked up slowly, his watery eyes focusing on the dark staircase above him. Had someone been listening. . . ? Could someone have snuck in and. . .

Loki bounded up the stairs, taking all four stories with ease. At the top he saw that Gaia's bedroom door was open. But all that greeted him inside was a wide-open window and billowing curtains.

The girl had been here, and now she was gone.

TOM HAD BEEN INSIDE SOME BAD

Glossy White Walls

prisons in his life. His personal least favorite had been in Somalia—it had had tarantulas the size of kittens—but the one in Bosnia had been nearly as bad because rotting corpses were left in their cells. The one he inhabited in Cuba had been relatively nice. The prison was in an abandoned mansion, which made it both pretty and easy to escape from.

This one wasn't filthy. In fact, it was squeaky clean. Hotel Niven, Tom dubbed it immediately, in honor of the failed agent who had sent him here. It had the white-walled, antiseptic feeling of a hospital, with not a speck of dirt to be seen. There were no bars, just a Plexiglas wall. But there was also no window—instead of a single shaft of sunlight framed by crumbling brick, he had a vent the size of a business envelope. There was no way to see the outside world, no way to tell what time it was.

Tom was trapped.

He knew that being in solitary confinement drove most men to stark screaming madness, but he was better trained than that. He could go inside his own mind and pass the time by working out complicated algorithms or calling up the text of the Declaration of Independence. Techniques like these were one of the first things taught at training school. But he had a more pressing matter to wonder about.

Where was Natasha?

The six goons who had dumped him in here had given no hint that someone else had been captured, but one of them wore a walkie-talkie that had squawked while he was being dragged inside. He thought he'd heard her scream, but he couldn't be sure. One thing he did know: If George Niven was the snake, then Natasha was what he had always insisted she was—loyal and honest.

With a wave of guilt, he realized he was responsible for her capture as well.

There was no reason to stand. He had to conserve his strength. He sat, with his back against the wall and facing the Plexiglas, knees drawn up in front of him. He was probably being watched, though he couldn't see a pinhole for the camera. But he was surely being observed somehow.

So: With his hasty, thinking-with-his-heart move, he had jeopardized himself, Natasha, Gaia, and the entire mission. Was he really any better than George Niven? George had betrayed him maliciously; he had betrayed himself carelessly. The result was the same.

He supposed the glossy white walls repelled the stains of splattered blood.

Through the vent he heard a faint shuffling, then a louder series of thuds, uneven, like limbs flailing. Then a torrent of Russian curses. Then another thud, and the electric hum of Plexiglas being lowered.

Then Natasha was alive. And in another cell. Should he call to her?

Tom remained silent. He had already made one major mistake today. If the vent allowed him to hear Natasha, he had no doubt that was not an accident. To begin chatting with her over the internal air-conditioning system—that would be playing into his captor's hands.

He sat very still, trying not to even acknowledge that he'd heard anything.

He heard Natasha beat against the Plexiglas, making frustrated grunts. Then an exasperated sigh. He desperately wanted to speak, to say something comforting, at least to apologize. But he had been clumsy enough for one day. For now he had to be silent. For now he had to sit tight and think.

He was proud to note that from what he could tell, she never gave in to tears.

He wasn't so sure he'd be able to do the same.

HEATHER FELT LIKE SHE'D JUST

Fifty Feet Up

had the greatest spa treatment of her life. All the toxins had been sucked from her pores—except this time there was one very big toxin that she'd ditched, and it wasn't going to be back.

She'd had the fear-free seaweed wrap.

What was next—the bird/plane shampoo and

blowdry? The ESP-enhanced relaxation and mind-meld massage?

She was so amused by this train of thought, she let out a big cackle. Josh turned to her, squeezing her hand.

"Are you sure you're all right?" he asked for the umpteenth time as they walked toward the 7 train.

"I am *fine*," she told him, trying hard not to snap his head off. It was sweet that he was so worried about her. But it was also annoying. What was he so afraid of? She wasn't sure she liked this side of Mr. Cute. He was rapidly becoming Mr. Mother Hen. If that kept up, he was going to have to become Mr. Blown Off.

"So do you want me to take you home?" he asked. "Do you want to come to my place? I think you should rest." Make that Mr. So Blown Off.

"I don't need to rest," she insisted. "I don't want to go inside anywhere—that guy was asking me so many questions, he made my head spin. I want to take a long walk, clear my head, and figure out what's different about me. Take myself for a test-drive. Doesn't that make sense?"

"It does," Josh said. "Of course. How does it feel? Do you feel different?"

"I feel—I feel the same, sort of," Heather mused. "But better. It's like I had a toothache all my life and never realized it, and now that the pain is gone, I feel great. You know?"

"Yeah, I think so." Josh gave her that adorable grin, and Heather felt a little more relaxed. Maybe he could stick around. From where they were strolling, she had a good view of the inky black city, the skyscrapers rising out of it like long, gleaming fingers. A cruise ship motored through the choppy waves. And stretching across the East River. . .

"I have an idea," she said, grabbing Josh's hand. "There's something I always wanted to do. Come on!"

Josh had no choice but to follow her onto the subway, tooling first across Manhattan, then down on the 6 train. He watched Heather carefully. There didn't seem to be any ill effects: her skin looked healthy, she wasn't sweating, and her pupils weren't dilated. She was alert, smiling to herself, reading the ads on the nearly empty car over and over again. In fact, she looked better than she had in days—whatever the phobosan preparation pills were doing to her, the injection had alleviated the symptoms completely. She looked excited, as happy as a little girl on her way to the skating rink. But he had a feeling what was ahead of them was a little scarier than a Zamboni-smoothed block of ice.

"Here we go," she said, tugging on his arm at the Brooklyn Bridge stop.

"Heather, you've got to tell me what we're—"

"Come on! Move it or lose it." She stood and strode out of the car, and he had no choice but to follow her.

It was that or lose track of her completely. And he wanted to keep an eye on Heather—maybe to make sure "fearless" didn't also mean "careless."

"I've heard stories of people doing this," she said, walking confidently up the pedestrian ramp that spanned the bridge. During the day this was a favorite stroll for locals and tourists alike; the wooden-slatted walkway provided the best view of the city for free. At night it wasn't generally considered safe. And Josh had a feeling they weren't just out for an unpatrolled stroll.

"Wow, the city sure looks great from here," Josh said, in a valiant attempt at conversation.

"Sure, it looks nice from down here," Heather said. "But think how much better it'll look from *up there*." She pointed up into the dizzying heights of the sky, at the brick towers, the vaulted arches shaped like church doors, that stretched above them.

"Heather, you're not actually planning to. . ."

"Oh, I am." And without another word, she stepped onto the massive, gracefully curved metal tubes that connected the cables to the main structure. The one she was on went straight to the top of the tower; she could hold on to the cables with her hands, but the climb was dizzying. Thrill seekers failed with great regularity in their attempts to make it, either tumbling into the water or hanging on by a thread until the cops came, got them down, and arrested them. This was a dumb move. It was, in fact, idiotic. It was also fearless. That was clearly what Heather was trying to prove.

"Come on," she called out. She was already a quarter of the way up the tube, placing her feet carefully but without hesitation, and not even flinching when she looked down. "Please? It's not going to be any fun to be up there alone."

Heart pounding like a jackhammer, Josh began following her. He was bigger and had more strength, but she wasn't suffering from vertigo; he had to keep his eyes drilled onto her blue-jeaned butt to keep from falling off in total terror. Meanwhile Heather monkeyed up each step of the way without hesitation. When she reached the top, she ran around the large rim of the tower, laughing, spinning, and shouting at the city.

"Hello, Manhattan!" she shrieked. "Hello, you gorgeous, dirty old city. Do you see me up here? I'm Heather Gannis. *Heather Gannis!* And I'm not afraid of you—or anything else. You hear me? *You don't scare me anymore!*" Now she was shouting at the sky, her arms held out wide. Josh double-timed it up the rest of the way, afraid a gust of wind would carry her off the edge.

"All right. Are we done?" he asked. "You've proved your point. Now come down with me."

"Down? Are you crazy-nutso-cuckoo?" She laughed.

"I didn't ask you up here just to sightsee. There's something I want to do up here."

Oh, no. Please don't tell me, Josh thought. But sure enough, she strode toward him in an exaggerated imitation of a vixen and grabbed the fly of his jeans.

"Come on," she purred. "Give a girl a thrill."

But the sad truth was that Josh was really, really scared up there. And when a guy is scared, the plumbing just doesn't work. No matter what a girl does to try and fix it.

The smile vanished from Heather's face; her jaw dropped.

"You've got to be kidding me," she said.

"Sorry." Josh shrugged.

She let her hands fall to her sides and gave him a polite but clearly disappointed smile. "I was looking forward to this."

"Oh, come on." He put his arms around her and drew her in for a kiss, trying to ignore the fact that he was fifty feet up with no safety railing. "Hey, you can tell everybody we did. Who's going to know we didn't?"

She kissed him back, then turned around to view the city, wrapping his arms around her like a stole.

"It's spectacular," she said. "I never thought I'd see such a thing."

It was true: after the long, cold, arduous climb, the

winking lights of the city were even more beautiful, standing out in sharp contrast to the velvety black sky. Clear nights were hard to come by in New York City, but this one was perfect. Lines of headlights made twin strands of white and red pearls running down the side of Manhattan, along the FDR Drive. The water beneath them was an inky black expanse, a vacuum of enormous proportions. Behind them Brooklyn Heights stood quietly, the softly lit promenade glowing in the darkness. In the distance, the red-capped clock tower told four different versions of the time.

Josh tried to relax, but his body was humming with tension.

Not Heather's, though. He could feel how easy she was with this. And without warning she ran out of his grasp and leapt onto the tube again, taking the trip down in bounds and long slides that made his heart clench with terror for her. He heard wild laughter as she lost her footing and barely caught herself, recklessly swinging over the water.

"*Heather!*" he called out, throwing himself facedown on the bricks and peering over the edge as if he could reach down with Plastic Man arms and rescue her.

But all he heard in response was more of that laughter, floating up through the darkness as she raced down the bridge's cables, hitting the ground and running back to Manhattan before he could even brace himself to step over the edge onto the cables again.

Who knew what she'd do next? And Josh wouldn't be there to protect her. He'd gotten her infected with a fearless virus, and now he couldn't even manage to stay by her side.

With an oppressive wave of regret Josh realized he had manipulated an amazing girl—probably causing her irreparable damage. But it was worse than that. He had done this to a girl, it turned out, that he truly cared about. All his playacting had been so easy—because it was becoming real.

He had brought her into this mess. And Heather was the only girl he'd ever loved.

Wow. Oh, wow. OH, MAN.

This is so intense. I thought I was prepared for how this would feel. I was not. It's as if I just entered another dimension. Or switched bodies. That guy Oliver was right—I do feel like I'm in *The Matrix*.

My whole reality has shifted. I'm seeing the world through different eyes, and everything is so much sharper, clearer, more beautiful, more simple, more complex.

I'm not making any sense. This must be what it's like to have a religious conversion. The only way I can describe it is, I feel like I've finally become myself.

I fooled myself into thinking I was prepared for the injection, but looking back on the whole experience, man, was I freaked out. Those pills were awful. The withdrawal took so much out of me that I had no energy left to care about anything else. I wandered around town like a sleepwalking fashion emergency, and those last couple of times I saw Ed, I was practically speaking in tongues. On some level I was aware that I was turning into a freak show, but somehow it didn't matter to me—I just kept picturing what my new life would be like.

I kept promising myself it would be worth it. But in the back of my mind, I'd reserved a space for disappointment.

But there is no disappointment.

There are some things that surprised me at first. I haven't suddenly turned into a supergenius. I know I can't fly. I guess I've read too many comic books or something—I thought that if the injection worked, I'd be completely transformed. But I wasn't. I'm still me.

Heather Gannis, but better. And the old Heather was pretty damn good herself.

With this new, fearless attitude I know I can fix anything that goes wrong. I can deal with anything that comes up because

I'm not hemmed in by second
guessing. I'm not going to trip
myself up with doubt. And that is
so. . . amazing.

Those antidrug seminars they
give us at school used to scare
the pants off me. I thought I'd
go crazy and jump off a building
if I swallowed an extra Advil by
mistake. So when I agreed to that
injection, I considered the
possibility that it could turn me
into one of those ladies with a
tinfoil hat and seventeen stuffed
animals in a shopping cart, walking around the city talking about
how John F. Kennedy has stolen
their brain.

But I'm glad I pushed through
all my doubts.

Because this is the most
incredible thing that's ever happened to me.

I totally rock!

IT WAS FUNNY HOW FURY LIT A FIRE

under Tatiana's ass—and under Gaia's as well. As soon as she'd heard George admit he was a lying sack of garbage, Gaia had tried to leap forward, lunging out of the shadows to attack George and his shadowy associate. It was only Tatiana's urgent hand on her arm that had stopped her: Duh. If she did anything now, both their parents were dog meat.

Worse Than Duped

Getting down was a lot easier than climbing up. Gaia and Tatiana both swung out and down through the tree by the fire escape, acutely aware that if Loki caught them, they might as well climb into their coffins themselves. Down on the sidewalk they took off, running down the zigzagging West Village streets till they were well away from the brownstone. They finally stopped to catch their breath near Washington Square Park, Gaia's old stomping ground.

"I apologize," Gaia blurted. "I was totally and completely wrong to trust George. I can't believe I fell for his crap—again."

Danger that they hadn't seen, Gaia thought, because she'd been too trusting of George to look for it. Goddamn him. She wanted to scream with embarrassment, frustration, and anger. They'd all been duped—worse than duped. George had taken them for a bunch of suckers.

LOKI RETURNED DOWNSTAIRS, TAK-

Crystal Balls

ing each step with slow, considered deliberation. Surely it was his precious Gaia who had leapt from the window. He felt his mighty knot of a plan begin to fray at the edges and unravel. Gaia had been in the palm of his hand, and now she was running away from him again. The sloppiness of this situation filled him with a cold fury. A fury he could taste. He had Tom in his clutches and his troublesome cohort as well, but they were mere consolation prizes. Gaia was still out of his reach—and he had been so close.

At the bottom landing he could see George, still standing in the foyer, gazing into his drink as if the ice cubes were crystal balls. *This useless man,* Loki thought bitterly. *He is more trouble than he's worth.*

"She got away," George said, his voice no longer wavering from the alcohol. "It was Gaia. She heard every word and got away." Slowly he looked up, his eyes meeting Loki's.

"She was too clever for me after all," he said, some vestige of his old self glinting through the fog of his consciousness. "Too clever for you, too. You've involved me in your sick conspiracy—but you will never be able to twist her mind and involve her in your demented—"

But Loki wouldn't let George finish. He took three steps toward him and felt nothing as he emptied the barrel of his gun into the old man's forehead.

He stepped backward so that the body could fall, unhindered, to the ground, where it landed with an inhuman thump. Then he stepped over it and let himself out the front door.

Behind him the last oozing drops of George Niven's life seeped silently into the richly patterned Oriental rug.

There's this *Star Trek*
movie that came out when I was a
kid where they talk about the
Kobayashi Maru. Don't get me
wrong—I wasn't a complete and
total unrepentant nerd; I did not
see *Star Trek* of my own free
will. I went to keep my mother
company. That was her only weakness, I guess: cheesy sci-fi
movies. Anyway, the Kobiyashi
Maru was a no-win situation. It
was a test they gave all the
cadets at Starfleet Academy: Pose
a completely impossible situation, one where the outcome is
cataclysmic no matter what orders
they give, and judge them on
their poise and reactions.

   I feel like I just took the
stupid Kobayashi Maru. And I
don't think I did too well.
Anyway, I'm not happy about it.

   Was there a happy ending here?
Was there a resolution to the
who's-telling-the-truth situation
that would have made anyone
happy? At first I wanted to prove

that George was telling the truth
so that I could hurt Tatiana and
rid my life of her and her
mother. Then as Tatiana grew on
me, I just wanted to cure her of
her hopeful, positive view of the
world.

But is that what I was *really*
trying to do? Maybe what I truly
wanted was for George to be
telling the truth so that I could
prove that unpleasant as his
information might be, at least I
had one trustworthy soul in my
corner.

But of course, I didn't. I
haven't since my mother died.
Except for Ed. But whether or not
he's still in my corner remains
to be seen.

I should be happy, right? I
don't have to worry about Natasha
anymore, and it turns out
Tatiana's kind of cool in the
bargain. Maybe. Possibly accept-
able. And this fantasy I have,
the dream my dad painted in his
letters to Natasha, has a shot at
coming true.

But I can't even enjoy that.
Because you know what? George was
supposed to be a sure thing. Much
as I bucked his authority, much
as I hated being dumped in his
house and resented his attention,
at least he always seemed to have
my best interests at heart.
Seemed, of course, being the
operative word.

I wish I knew what snapped in
the old guy. I'd like to say it
was his own stupid weakness that
brought him here, but there's a
part of me that wonders if it
wasn't my fault. I was such an
unmitigated bitch. When he asked
me to live with him that last
time, was it so he could sell me
out to Loki?

Or was it just the final plea
of a lonely old guy who was tired
of being alone?

And when I refused him, did it
drive him over the edge?

No. That's so stupid. It
couldn't have been that simple.

Then again, maybe it could.
Maybe I broke this old man and

put my own father in the hands of
Loki.

Whoever's fault it is, I could
wring George's neck with my bare
hands.

Nobody's ever going to get me
to trust them like that again.

here is a
sneak peek of
Fearless™ #23:
FEAR

It's always a guy. A boy, really. Bubble boy.

You see them on TV sometimes, or read about them in books, or maybe you've just listened to the millions of lame jokes, but you get the basic idea. Boy. In bubble.

They have to stay in the bubble because they were born with this genetic problem. One of their genes got dinged in a certain way that keeps them from having an immune system. It's kind of like being born with AIDS, but even worse. These guys can die from anything. Bad cold? Dead. Flu? Dead. Mumps? Dead. Dead. Dead. All kinds of germs that don't even make a normal person sick at all can kill them before anyone even figures out what's wrong.

The only way these guys can stay alive is to keep a wall between them and the rest of the world. They can't ever touch another person without wearing some kind of big plastic gloves.

No hugs from mom. No kisses on the cheek. No way can they go to school. School is the Hot Zone for germs.

People can be right next to them, all around them, but they can never touch. There's always that wall, the wall between the bubble boys and the rest of the world. Keeping them isolated. Keeping them alive.

Here's a scientific fact for the day: The reason it's almost always a bubble boy is because that busted gene is on the X chromosome. Guys only have one of those. Screw it up and they're screwed for good. Girls come equipped with two. Break one, and there's a backup. Not too many bubble girls. Not too many bubble men either—they usually don't live that long.

So, whatever is wrong with me, it's probably not a bad X chromosome. Maybe it *is* genetic. Maybe not. I've been led down the wrong road so many different times. Daddy gave you bad drugs, Gaia.

Daddy went all Jurassic Park on your genes, Gaia. Daddy built little Franken-Gaia with a blow-torch and some spare parts. Who knows what to believe? Who cares?

Whatever caused me to be the way I am, I've ended up as the opposite of a bubble boy. I don't mean I can't get sick. Show me a cold virus and I can produce more snot than a rhino. The only thing I'm completely immune to is fear. Never felt it, probably never will. I still need that bubble, though. A nice, safe barrier between me and the rest of the world. Not to protect me. To pro-tect the world.

See, it's not me who dies when I get touched, it's everyone else. My mom? Dead. Sam, the first guy I ever really loved. Dead. Mary, my best friend. Dead. Dead. Dead.

It could be that they all died of the same disease. A disease that walks on two legs and goes by the name of Loki. A disease that's also my uncle.

But if Loki is the disease, I'm the carrier. I take the infection out to the rest of the world.

Even with the population of Gaia's personal graveyard always on the rise, there are still a few people in the world that I care about.

There's my father. My always missing father. He knows more about what's going on than he will tell me, which is a good reason to hate him. And I do. Sometimes. But even when I'm busy hating him, I still love him. I think. Anyway, at the moment he's off in God knows where doing God knows what and probably in danger.

There's Tatiana. She's not part of my family or anything—at least, not yet. It's not like she's my best friend, either. But lately she's been helping me figure out whatever's going on with her mom and my dad. The two of them might be missing together, which could be good for them because I know my dad is in love with Tatiana's mother. That is,

if both of them are still alive.
So I care about Tatiana, at least
a little.

But the biggest reason I have
to stay in the Gaia bubble is Ed.
Ed, the first guy I ever had sex
with. Ed, the guy I still love.
Ed, the guy I've managed to piss
off for weeks now. Ed, the guy
that poured out his heart to me
and left convinced that I didn't
care. That Ed.

By now, Ed has probably written me off as a lost cause.
Tatiana has a black belt in
flirting and she's been using all
her best moves on Ed. The two of
them have been spending a lot of
time together. I know Ed's gone
completely MIA on her for the
last couple of days, but wherever
he's been hiding, I'll bet that
the next time I see him, he'll be
in Tatiana's arms. And that's
good. That's what I want, the way
it has to be. That's the plastic
bubble that protects Ed from the
disease I'm carrying.

But why does it have to feel

so miserable? So I can work up a
good, self-righteous "I'm doing
this to protect him" kind of
feeling? That feeling, as they
say, will not keep me warm on a
cold night.

Doesn't matter. Until this is
all over, I've got to stay inside
my chilly little bubble. Look, but
don't touch. See, but don't feel.

The Amazing Bubble Girl, keeping the world safe from myself.

Playing happy was not exactly a Gaia Moore specialty. Turning every **smears** hurt into anger **and** and making a solid **streaks** fist-to-face connection, that was more her style.

THE PHONE RANG A FOURTH TIME.

Fifth. Gaia thumped her hand against the metal pay phone and listened as a sixth ring came from the other end. She could picture the old wall phone ringing in the kitchen of the brownstone, the sound echoing off all the expensive— and unused cookware. She could see the curving staircase. Was the house completely empty, or was old

Clammy Empty Quiet

George Niven stumbling down those stairs toward the phone? George had been there only hours before. Gaia and Tatiana had seen him. Maybe he was just about to answer. Gaia let the phone ring one more time.

Come on, Georgie. Pick up.

The phone rang two more times. Gaia sighed and was about to hang up, when the receiver made a sudden click.

"Hello there," said a woman's voice. The tone was cool, self-possessed. "I'm afraid that we can't take your call at the moment. Please leave. . ."

Gaia hung up the pay phone before the message could end. It was Ella. The voice on the answering machine was George's wife Ella. Only Ella Niven had been dead for months. A little tingly feeling went up the back of Gaia's neck, once again demonstrating that just because you didn't feel fear, that didn't mean you couldn't be solidly creeped

10

out. Wasn't George ever going to get around to changing the message? It was kind of sweet that he had left his wife's voice on the phone. It was also pretty sick.

For a few seconds, Gaia stood and looked at the pay phone. She thought about calling again, but she didn't want to take the chance of hearing Ella's voice a second time. Hearing Ella had never been a blast when she was alive. Hearing her dead. . . That was a thrill Gaia would just as soon skip, thank you.

She flipped the hood up on her sweatshirt, hunched her shoulders, and walked away from the phone booth. A businesswoman went past on her left, followed by a college-age guy in some ridiculous parka thing that looked like something you would wear on top of the Matterhorn instead of in lower Manhattan. Gaia gave them both a quick once-over as they passed. Were they part of Loki's organization? Was one of them following Gaia, making notes about her, reporting on her ever move? Somebody was. Gaia knew that much.

Loki's agents were out there. Tracking where she went. Who she saw. When she came in, when she went out. Probably taking notes on what kind of Jell-O she had for lunch at the stupid school cafeteria.

Of course, the first one to tell Gaia that she was being followed had been George Niven. So maybe she really wasn't being followed. After all, everything else George had told her had been a big, fat, slimy sack of lies.

Gaia had bought into all of it at first. That was the worst part, how quickly she had swallowed the whole story. But why shouldn't she? Good old George was her father's best and oldest friend. He was going to help Gaia. He was going to help her catch the bad guys. Good old trustworthy George.

Only George was one of the bad guys. George had told her that Tatiana's mother, Natasha, had been the enemy. That Natasha had been spying on Gaia's father. And Gaia had believed it. Even after she'd found a stack of love letters between her father and Natasha, Gaia had still been ready to believe George. She had been willing to do anything, even hurt Natasha or Tatiana, to protect her father. She had been stupid on a galactic scale.

If it hadn't been for Tatiana, Gaia would have still been convinced that George was trying to help. Gaia had never doubted which side George was on. Come on, George Niven? Best friend and mentor to her father? The same George Niven whose brownstone Gaia had lived in for months? Paunchy, gray-haired, harmless, old George? George could be clueless, sure, but no way could he be on the Dark Side. That wasn't possible.

Okay, so maybe buying into the lies wasn't the worst part. Having Tatiana prove her wrong; that was the worst part.

Tatiana had not been fooled by good old George. No matter what Gaia said, she hadn't trusted the ex-agent.

Tatiana had badgered and pleaded and whined until she finally got Gaia to agree to make a trip to George's brownstone. The only reason Gaia had gone there was to prove once and for all that she was right, that Tatiana was wrong, and that Tatiana should just shut up. Only that wasn't how it had worked out.

When they'd snuck through the window of the room that used to be Gaia's bedroom, they had gotten a glimpse of a meeting between good old George and the seriously un-good Loki. Maybe George had been a friend to Gaia's father once. Maybe he had even been a friend to Gaia. That wasn't true anymore. George was working for Loki and lying to Gaia.

So maybe there wasn't anybody following Gaia. Maybe that was all part of the big pile of steaming hot crap that George had put in Gaia's eager hands. Maybe Loki was laughing somewhere about making Gaia look over her shoulder. After all, it was perfectly obvious that George had been lying to her from the start.

But Gaia didn't think so. Not this time. The part about being followed every moment of her life. That part Gaia still believed.

It had rained that morning, and the sidewalks were still splotched with puddles. Gaia hopped over a wide, muddy spot and managed to keep from getting her sneakers soaked. Then a car went past on the street and sent a wave of oily water washing across her feet. Gaia gave the driver a glance. The guy behind the wheel looked weird, but half the people in the city were weird. This guy in a Buick probably wasn't keeping a Gaia notebook, and he probably hadn't gotten her shoes wet on Loki's orders. Probably. But even paranoids had enemies. Gaia tromped on down the damp sidewalk toward the park.

This whole phone call thing had probably been a bad idea. The latest in a long series of Gaia's Really Bad Ideas. She knew that, really. If Gaia had actually believed calling George was a good idea, she would have done it from the apartment. She would have had Tatiana on the other line so they could talk about it. She wouldn't have left Tatiana snoozing and snuck out to make the call from some pay phone.

After all, how smart was it to call the guy you just found out was setting you up? But Gaia was hoping that, if she could convince George that she was still in the dark, she could turn this thing around. If he didn't know that he had been caught with Loki, Gaia might be able to feed him bad information, get him to make mistakes, maybe even get him to spill something about what had really happened to her father and Natasha.

Gaia squeezed her eyes shut and stood still for a moment. Just trying to think it through was enough to make her head hurt. Anyway, it was hard to pass bad information to someone if they wouldn't even answer the phone.

She walked across the street and slipped into

Washington Square Park. She fought the temptation to look over her shoulder as she passed through the gates. If people were following her, they were probably pretty good at it. After all, they had been following her for months and she hadn't seen them yet. It wasn't like they were suddenly going to start waving or carrying signs that said, "I'm following Stupid." Gaia kept her face forward and kept walking.

The chess players were mostly gone from their place near the center of the park, and the few who were still at their tables seemed deep in the endgames of long matches. Gaia skirted around the area anyway. She didn't want to play at the moment and didn't want to deal with Zolov, or Mr. Pak, or anyone else who might be looking for a late game. She had to think. She had to figure out the next step.

She thought about going back to the East Side apartment and meeting Tatiana. Together, they might have a better shot at coming up with a plan. After all, it was Tatiana who had figured out the truth about George. Maybe she would have some good ideas. Something better than playing phone tag with the enemy.

But Gaia didn't go home. She just kept marching.

Part of it was that she wasn't ready to meet with Tatiana. Part of it was that she liked walking — it was what she did when the she needed to think. Most of it was that she had been doing things on her own for so long that it was hard to change. The last person she had trusted had been George, and that had been a big mistake. Once you convinced yourself that you couldn't trust anyone, how did you ever start trusting again?

Without planning to, Gaia found herself coming out the north side of the park and turning toward George's brownstone. She wasn't sure she really wanted to confront the old agent face-to-face. She definitely wanted to try her plan of passing along misinformation, but there was one big problem with that plan — she wasn't sure she could look at George without trying to remove his head from his shoulders. He had lied to her. He had betrayed her father. He was helping Loki. For all Gaia knew, George might even have been involved in the deaths of Sam and Mary.

Convincing George that they were still pals was going to mean swallowing a lot of anger and not letting it show. It was going to take some serious acting. Gaia wasn't sure she was up to it. Hiding her feelings and playing happy was not exactly a Gaia Moore specialty. Turning every hurt into anger and making a solid fist-to-face connection, that was more her style.

Gaia was still over a block from George's place when she spotted something wrong. There was something in front of the house, something yellow. From that distance, Gaia couldn't tell quite what it was she was looking at, but as she walked slowly up the block, it became clear. Yellow tape. Police tape. The front of the brownstone was blocked off with a double line of police tape.

Gaia stood across the street with her hands shoved down into the pocket of her sweatshirt and watched as the tape fluttered in the chill, damp breeze.

If the brownstone was marked off with police tape, then it had to be a crime scene. Gaia supposed there could have been a burglary or a robbery. Ella had stocked the brownstone with several ugly but expensive bits of art. Some thief with equally bad taste might have broken in for that. But Gaia didn't think so. She didn't think the police would have taped off the entrance if it had been a robbery. This had to be... something worse.

Gaia stayed on the sidewalk and watched the house for a few minutes as the sun slipped behind the taller buildings on the far side of the park and the cars rolling slowly down the street turned on their lights. She turned around to leave, took a couple of steps, then turned again and marched through the traffic to the front steps of the brownstone.

Close up, it was easier to read the words on the yellow banner.

NYPD CRIME SCENE INVESTIGATIONS
DO NOT CROSS

Gaia took the plastic tape in her hands and snapped it. The two ends fluttered away as she stepped to the door and took the knob in her hand. It was locked, of course. The NYPD wouldn't want thieves breaking in and messing up their nice clean crime scene.

It wasn't a problem for Gaia. She fished in her pocket and came out with a single key. She slotted it into the door and turned the knob again. This time, it opened with a soft click. It figured that if George wasn't even going to change his answering machine message after his wife's death, he wasn't going to change the lock on the front door just because Gaia had moved out.

It was weird stepping inside. It was always strange to go back to some place where you used to live. Gaia almost expected to see herself coming down the stairs, like the brownstone was some kind of three-story time machine. But she didn't see her past self, or the ghost of Ella, or George. The front hallway was dark and quiet.

Gaia closed the front door and walked on into the living room. There was a light on beside the couch, but the room still seemed to swarm with shadows. Could a house get haunted overnight? Gaia could hear the soft hum of the refrigerator purring in the kitchen. It was a comforting sound. The brownstone was still, in some way, alive. But the fridge seemed to be the only living thing in the house.

It was cold. Either the refrigerator was working overtime or the heat was busted. The temperature inside the house didn't seem much warmer than it had outside. It was damp, too. Clammy. That was the right word. The inside of the brownstone was way clammy.

Gaia finished a lap around the lower rooms without seeing anything wrong. She took a chance and turned on some additional lights in the kitchen and hall. The lights drove away the shadows but didn't give any clue about what had happened. The books were still on the shelves. Ella's ugly postmodern prints were still hanging on the walls. There were a couple of dirty glasses on the counter beside the sink, but it was obvious that George had been keeping the place neat. There was no sign of theft. Or a fight. Or anything. Just the clammy empty quiet.

The bedrooms on the second floor were much the same. Everything neat. Everything in its place.

Gaia stopped again on the landing leading up to the top floor. It was dark at the top of the stairs, but the room up there was so absolutely familiar, Gaia could have walked through it with her eyes closed. It was the room where she had lived for the months she'd spent here with George and Ella. It was the same room that she and Tatiana had climbed into the night before. It was a place she had seen a thousand times.

But for almost a minute, Gaia just stood there and looked up the stairs as if they led to some alien world. She wasn't afraid of what she would find. She just didn't know if she'd like it.

She walked up the stairs to her old bedroom. There

was another strand of police tape here, strung across the bedroom door. Gaia looked past it into the room. The lights were off, and Gaia made no move to turn them on. The only light in the bedroom came from the streetlights streaming through the window. It was dim enough that it took her a few seconds to realize that the window was open. The white curtains moved slowly in the cold breeze. That explained the cold and damp—the clammy—feeling in the brownstone.

The open window was the same one that Gaia and Tatiana had used to get into the apartment. Had they left it open when they'd escaped? Gaia couldn't remember. If they had left it open, then why hadn't George closed it?

Gaia's eyes slowly adjusted to the dimly lit space. She began to make out more details in the room. Most of it was still the way it had been when she'd lived there. The bed was still in its place. The other furniture hadn't changed. But there was one big difference. In the middle of the floor was an outline made from short strips of white tape.

The outline of a human body.

Something ran along Gaia's spine that was far bigger than a shiver. This was more like some kind of convulsion. Her throat tightened painfully and tears pushed against her eyes. Gaia stepped into the room, barely noticing the length of yellow crime scene tape as it pulled away from the door frame. The body outlined on the floor was clearly that of an adult man. The tape showed where one hand was thrown back behind the head. The other was pressed against the chest. From the shape, it was clear that the body had been big, maybe a little overweight. It had to be the outline of George Niven.

Oh God, George. Gaia angrily rubbed at her eyes and shook her head. *No.* She wasn't going to be sorry for George.

In the middle of the outlined form was a dark stain that was nearly invisible in the poor light. Gaia crouched down beside the taped figure and reached toward the dark spot at the center. Her hand was trembling. Not with fear, but with some emotion she couldn't even name.

George was a traitor. He had gone against her father, given information to Loki, and lied to Gaia. She shouldn't feel any sympathy for him. Rats got killed. Nobody cried over the rats. It didn't matter why George had done the...

"Wow," said a voice behind her. "Look at that."

Gaia jumped to her feet and turned. She had her arms ready, her hands formed into curving blades and her muscles tensed to attack. She was expecting Loki, expecting one of his goons, expecting anything. Okay, almost anything. She was not expecting what she saw.

Standing in the door of the bedroom was a dark form lit by the light from below. The form was slender, a girl's form. Gaia could just make out thick, shoulder-length dark hair that hung in a loose, uncombed tumble. The shadowed contours of a face.

"Heather?"

The bedroom lights came on with a snap. Gaia winced and squinted against the sudden brightness.

The girl in the doorway was Heather Gannis. Or at least, she looked like Heather. But not the Heather that Gaia knew. Heather had always been picture perfect. Perfect hair. Perfect clothes. Any time Gaia spent with Heather made her feel like something found under a rock. But this girl. . . this girl made Gaia look neat.

Heather's hair was a mass of untamed brunette strands guaranteed to break the toughest comb. Her jeans were ripped out at one knee. Her worn gray sweater was muddy at the elbows and flecked with bits of dried leaves. There was a dark smudge across her face that might have been smeared makeup, but looked more like plain, old-fashioned dirt.

"Surprise," said Heather. She favored Gaia with a big, lopsided very un-Heather smile.

Gaia relaxed her fighting stance. "What are you doing here?"

"Me? I'm being a good citizen." Heather stepped into the room and paced slowly across the floor. "I saw someone breaking into a house. A crime scene no less. That seems like something any good citizen should stop." She scuffed her toe across the carpet. "Pretty messy in here, huh?"

Gaia looked down. What had been only a dark

stain with the lights off was clearly blood. And not just a little blood. The floor was dotted with fine fans of blood, as if someone had taken a can of spray paint and given the carpet a couple of good shots. It wasn't red like on TV. The blood had darkened, turning a deep brown that was almost black, but Gaia didn't have any doubt about what it was. There were little smears of the dried blood on the sides of her sneakers.

"Just look at this," said Heather. "What kind of housekeepers are these people?"

"The dead kind," Gaia replied. She stared at Heather's face, trying to get some clue about what was going on. Heather might be a world-class pain in the butt, and she might think the world revolved around her, but usually she demonstrated at least a tablespoon of sanity. "Are you on some kind of drug?"

Heather laughed. "Yeah, I guess you could say that. Or maybe it's that I'm the only one off drugs. A drug that makes everybody else act nuts." She walked into the center of the bedroom and started to circle around the outline on the floor.

"Right. Sure. You're the sane one." It was starting to seem like a good time to hide the sharp objects. "So, how did you get here?"

"Same way you did. Walked through the park. Took a little stroll along the sidewalk." Heather scuffed at the outline of George Niven's left arm. "I followed you."

23

Gaia scowled. "Followed me?" If Loki still sent his people to follow her and Heather followed her, did that mean there was a whole line of people behind her? "Why would you do that?"

"To show you I could. A little test. And I passed it. See what I'm saying, sister?"

"Sister?" Was she kidding? It had to be some kind of sick joke.

Heather kicked more tape from the floor. "I followed you to this place, and it was easy. So, so easy." She closed her eyes and smiled again.

Gaia felt a little angry that Heather had been out there following her. Angry at herself, mostly. After all, if she couldn't spot Heather Gannis stumbling along after her, what chance did she have of catching Loki's agents?

But anger wasn't the main thing Gaia was feeling. Something was wrong with Heather. Seriously wrong. "Listen," said Gaia, "you need to get out of here and stop following me around. It's dangerous."

"Dangerous? What do I care about dangerous?" Heather started circling the room again, moving more quickly this time. She waved her arms in the air to accent her words. "What do you think I am, some mouse? That's what you think, isn't it? You think I'm a mouse."

"Mouse?" Gaia started to feel dizzy as she spun to face Heather. The nearly dry blood squished under her feet. The taped outline of George Niven was being torn apart. Heather's arms went up and down. Her shadow on the wall seemed alien. Inhuman. The whole thing suddenly didn't feel like any kind of joke. It felt more like a scene from a nightmare. Madness and violence. Blood and shadows.

"Heather." Gaia reached out to stop Heather, but the dark-haired girl batted Gaia's hands away.

"You're right," said Heather. "You're right about the following. I shouldn't be following you now. It's too late for that." She danced across the head of the tape outline, tearing up the few pieces that were still attached to the floor. "I shouldn't be following anyone."

"Heather, stop." Gaia reached out again. This time, Heather didn't push her hands away. This time the girl unloaded with a looping, right-handed punch that caught Gaia just in front of her ear.

Gaia had been punched a hundred times. Probably more like a thousand. But no punch ever caught her so much by surprise. She hadn't expected Heather to hit her. She had never expected Heather to hit *anyone*. And she hadn't expected Heather to be so fast or so strong.

Gaia went to her knees on the blood-soaked floor. Her ears rang from the impact. Since when was Heather Gannis able to hit like that? Gaia looked up to see Heather standing in the doorway. Heather's face was tilted down and her tangled hair shadowed her features, but Gaia could still see the smile on Heather's lips.

"I'm all through following," said Heather. "From now on, I'm going to take the lead."

25

"You're going to lead all right," said Gaia. She stood up and looked down at the stains on her jeans. There was blood, human blood, all over her. "You're going to lead the way right to the land of rubber rooms and straitjackets."

There was a noise from the hallway. When Gaia looked up, Heather was gone. A moment later, she heard footsteps moving rapidly down the stairs, followed by the slamming of the brownstone's front steps.

Gaia took one last look around the room. Everywhere there were smears and streaks of the brownish, nearly dry blood. The outline that had looked so like a human figure a few minutes ago was now meaningless, scattered bits of tape spread all over the flood. The scene looked terrible enough to Gaia. How would it look to anyone else? How would it look to the police? What are you doing in this room, Ms. Moore? How did you get into this brownstone? Were you returning to the scene of the crime? Where were you at the time of the murder?

These were not questions Gaia was in a big hurry to answer. All at once, her stomach took a major elevator ride toward her throat and Gaia had to press a hand over her mouth to keep from throwing up. The way the tape was torn up, the way the blood was splattered. It made it look like. . . not a murder. A massacre. Like someone had been torn to pieces in the apartment.

Gaia fled from the room and tore down the steps so fast she nearly broke her own neck before she made it to the main floor. She went out the door, not worrying about whether she bothered to lock the brownstone behind her. If someone stole Ella's bad-taste collection now, what difference would it make?

A cold tear ran down Gaia's cheek and she brushed it away angrily. George had betrayed her. He had betrayed her father. He didn't deserve her tears. Only... had he really deserved to die?

Gaia took deep breaths as she ran. They helped to calm her stomach. Too bad they didn't do so much for her head. What had happened to George? Had Loki double-crossed him? Or had he suspected that George was telling Gaia more than he was supposed to?

There were way too many questions and not enough answers... and the list of people that might be able to give her some of the answers was getting shorter all the time.

THE SUN HAD BEEN DOWN FOR

Between Miami and Martinique

nearly an hour, but there was still a blur of deep violet light on the western horizon. The light shimmered across the slowly heaving sea and lit up the breakers as

27

they smashed against the nearby bluffs. It was a beautiful scene, really. A glorious tropical evening with sea and sand and waves. Only Tom Moore was not in the best of positions to enjoy the view.

He grabbed the bars on his cell window, braced his feet against the stone wall, and pulled. At first, the rusty iron gave a slight, encouraging movement, but then it settled down and refused to move again. Tom pulled until the veins were bulging on his arms and sweat ran down his forehead into his eyes. It was no use. The bars were not going anywhere without a big file or a stick of dynamite.

Tom let go of the bars and brushed the rust flakes off against his torn, dusty pants leg. He wasn't sure how long he had been in this place or how he had gotten here. At first, Loki's forces had held him in another, smaller cell. The last thing he remembered had been an injection, then darkness, and now this place. Since awakening on the creaking metal bunk in the corner of the cell, Tom had not seen any sign of a guard—or of anyone else. He might have been out for days or weeks—or for only minutes. He rubbed his hand across his chin. There was stubble there, but it was not too bad. Days. Call it two days.

He was somewhat surprised at still being held prisoner after this long. Not because he had expected Loki to let him go. Far from it. He was only surprised that he hadn't been killed. With all the rage that his brother had displayed over the years, Tom had expected no mercy at his hands.

What did Loki hope to gain by keeping Tom prisoner? Was he hoping to extract information? Was he planning some kind of torture? Tom couldn't be sure. He had never understood his brother's twisted desires. He wasn't going to try to understand them now.

The fact that he was alive meant that there was still hope. Hope for himself, but more importantly, hope for Natasha. Natasha had been taken prisoner along with Tom. She had been alive when Tom was moved to this place. If Tom had not been killed, there was every chance that Natasha had also been spared. She might even be being held in the same place where Tom was a prisoner. Wherever that was.

Tom turned away from the window and examined his cell again. The room was small, no more than two steps in either direction. The stone walls had been worn down by time and rain and the salt air, but they were still strong enough to prevent escape. The door was wood, which seemed to offer some chance that it might be broken, but this door was as thick as Tom's fist and so old that the wood seemed almost petrified. When he pounded against it, the sound was muffled and the door shook not at all. Not very promising.

Tom craned his head back and looked up. High above, there was a wide gap in the ceiling of the room. Through it, he could see a spray of stars across the night sky. If Tom could climb up to the opening, he could easily fit through the space and slip over the walls. Only the ceiling looked to be at least eighteen feet high, and the worn sandstone walls offered little chance for a handhold. Besides, the opening was not against the walls—it was in the middle of the room, with at least a couple of feet of solid roof on all sides.

He scanned the room. There was the cot. Six feet long. Maybe six and a half. There was a metal bucket. Another foot. If Tom were able to stand on top of the whole mess and put his arms overhead, he could reach up. . . maybe fifteen feet. That was five feet short of his goal.

Tom dragged the cot over to the middle of the room and tipped it up on edge. The little bed was made from aluminum tubing, and it looked none too sturdy turned up on end. Still, he grabbed the bucket, clenched the handle between his teeth, and climbed carefully to the top. The cot swayed precariously, and one of the metal tubes buckled slightly under Tom's weight, but it held. He balanced on one foot while he set the bucket on the end of the cot, then held out his arms for balance as he stepped onto the bucket. Finally, he looked up.

He could see the opening, so tantalizingly close, but so painfully far from reach. The distance between Tom's upraised fingertips and the edge of the opening was only three or four feet. From the ground, a standing jump of that distance would have been extremely tough. From here, perched on a tower of rickety metal, it was nearly impossible. And if he missed, it would be a long, painful drop to the stone floor of the cell.

Tom squinted. There was something at the edge of the opening. A broken spike that had once blocked the opening. With the cot and bucket trembling below him, Tom unbuttoned his stained white shirt and held it by the end of one sleeve. He took a deep breath, bent his knees, and leaped.

The cot and the bucket went tumbling away with a clatter of metal. Tom soared toward the opening, his hands coming within a foot of the corroded spike. . . but then he began to fall. At that moment, just as gravity started to drag him down toward the stones, Tom flung the shirt upward. The cloth tangled around the rusty metal, the sleeve whipping around and around.

There was a jerk, a shower of stone chips and rust, and an ominous tearing sound. Then Tom was dangling by one hand from the length of cloth.

He glanced down only for a moment. The floor of the cell was completely invisible in the gloom. He turned his attention upward and climbed hand over hand up the cotton shirt. The broken bit of metal dug into the flesh of Tom's chest as he squeezed past, but there was enough room. After a few anxious seconds, he was standing on the stone roof above his cell. The first stage of his escape had been accomplished.

Now that he was outside, he had a better idea of where he had been taken. The stone cell was just one small part of a rambling, tumbledown construction that covered most of a small island. There were the broken remains of a wall, several small buildings that had collapsed into heaps of worn stone block, and a large, central place that included the cell.

It was a fort of some kind. A hundred—probably hundreds of years old fort. Tom guessed that the building had been constructed by the Spanish or some other old colonial power to defend their holdings and shipping routes in the Caribbean. Whoever had built the place had picked an obscure spot. The island was no more than half a mile across, and as far as Tom could see, there was not another speck of land in sight. There was no clue as to where the island might lie. It could be close to the Caymans, or a thousand miles away. It might be anywhere between Miami and Martinique, Cuba and Caracas.

This was going to add another level of complexity to escaping. Getting out of his cell wasn't going to do much good unless he could also find a way off the island.

Tom walked across the roof. Thirty yards along, he came to another small opening. He went to it slowly and leaned down to look inside. Darkness.

"Natasha?" he called softly. "Natasha, are you down there?" There was no reply.

It was the same at the next opening. At the third opening, Tom heard movement even before he spoke. "Natasha?"

"Tom!" A shadow moved in the darkness. From the shadows below, Tom could see a pale face looking up.

"Are you all right?" She asked.

"I'm fine," Tom called down. Though he knew Natasha was too far away to see him, Tom couldn't help but smile. Knowing that she was close and uninjured, even if she was still captive, was enough to make him feel happier than he had in days. "Listen," he said. "I'm going to go and look for some rope or something that I can lower down to you."

"All right," said Natasha. "Be careful."

"Don't worry, we'll be out of here and on our way back to New York in ten minutes."

Tom stood up and turned around just in time to catch the wooden stock of a Kalashnikov rifle across his face. Then he was falling. Falling deep into blackness.

Gaia was gone when I woke up this morning. I don't know where she is, but I get the feeling she didn't just go out for a doughnut. Not this time. After what we saw last night, she knows that I was right. She knows that her father's friend was no friend at all.

My mother is not the enemy. She never was. I never doubted it, and now Gaia knows that it is true. I don't know how my mother ever got involved with someone like Gaia's father, but I knew she wasn't doing anything wrong. I knew it.

I only wish I knew where Gaia was right now. I'm really afraid that she's out doing something stupid. Ever since I got to this city, it seems like Gaia has been either doing something stupid or getting ready to do something stupid.

She's actually very smart. I know that. But it's amazing how stupid smart people can be when

they try, and Gaia's really been
trying. She's been pushing everyone away at the one time she
could use some help. That's
pretty stupid. She's been pushing
Ed away when he wants so much to
love her. That's terribly stupid.
I only hope that this time, for
once, Gaia is not out there doing
something too stupid. I hope that
she's not out attacking this Loki
or getting in trouble or getting
herself killed.

Gaia is smart, and she's
strong, and she can fight. If I'm
going to get my mother back, I'm
going to need Gaia's help. So
please, just this once, don't let
her be stupid.

Everyone's got his demons....

ANGEL™

If it takes an eternity, he will make amends.

❖

Original stories based
on the TV show
Created by Joss Whedon
& David Greenwalt

Available from Simon Pulse
Published by Simon & Schuster

SIMON
PULSE

BASED ON THE HIT TV SERIES

Charmed™

Prue, Piper, and Phoebe Halliwell didn't think the magical incantation would really work. But it did. Now Prue can move things with her mind, Piper can freeze time, and Phoebe can see the future. They are the most powerful of witches— the Charmed Ones.

Available from Simon & Schuster

2387